Children of Shadows

Charles Thorn

Children of Shadows

Acknowledgements

First and foremost I am indebted to my wife, Carole, for her encouragement and patience as this tale came together. Without her support I suspect this would have been just one more unfinished novel.

Many others have offered their knowledge, suggestions, and expertise. There are far too many to list, but I would particularly like to thank the following: Authors Kathryn Wall and Vicky Hunning, my brother, Bill Thorn, Ellie Kyle, Dahris Lawrence, Steve and Eileen Wholley, Lancy and Emily Burn, Chase Allen, Roger Pinckney XI, Greg Hutton, Pat Beichler, Freddie Grant, Deputy Chief Randall Osterman of Hilton Head Island Fire and Rescue, Connie Nienaber, and Captain Frankie Toomer of the shrimper "Yellow Jacket". Thanks also to Mike Pace, a fellow captain, friend, musician, and repository of the "Beatles" legacy.

I would be remiss not to mention mystical Daufuskie Island, South Carolina, my inspiration for the setting of much of the story. It is a place unlike any other I have known. My hope is that it will be spared the scourge of rampant development in the future.

Charlie Thorn
cthorn@aol.com

What Readers Are Saying:

"It is well-written with an interesting, fast-paced plot. Having been on your tour I was able to picture the setting which made it all the more enjoyable."
~ Susan Green

"You had a little bit of everything, such as action, romance, and mystery which made it a good read."
~ Kay Marshall

"I thoroughly enjoyed the book. I hope I get to read something of yours again."
~ Nina Jones

"Just finished reading "Children of Shadows". I loved it. Hopefully Cooper, Kathleen and Twilight will be back."
~ Faye Cosby

"I have finished your wonderful book. I truly didn't want it to end. You kept my interest from page one. The characters were amazing, and I told my husband that I could see it as a movie."
~ Cyndi Loomis

"We are listening to it now on Kindle as I am legally blind. It is very good."
~ Marty Stahlman

"When we returned home I read your novel, Children of Shadows. I really enjoyed it. I did not want to put it down. You brought the characters to life with great emotion."
~ Bill Webb

"We downloaded your book right away and Lisa read it on the plane. She says it's great and very well written. I am still busy with two other books but will definitely read it soon."
~ Anne Cattanach

"I had the opportunity to read your novel while travelling this week. The book is great, and your power of description is wonderful. In the event that you publish another, please let me know. I will certainly buy a copy."
~ Jim Zack

Part One

CHAPTER ONE

"I ain't waitin' no longer. She's gotta go," said Fletcher. His bulk slumped in the chair, and his elbows rested on the table. His right hand and forearm pivoted upwards as he lifted a glass to his lips. "Fit as she is, she could last another ten or fifteen years."

Craig Wellons, the taller of the two men seated with him, shook his head. "Sonny you're talkin' . . ."

"Bullshit. I ain't talking about nothin' but a old woman dyin' in her sleep. That's all there is to it."

"Well, how do we make that happen?"

When Fletcher leaned forward his badge brushed against the edge of the table. Sweat rimmed his collar, and his double chin rolled with his words. He looked at the third man and said, "Go get a pencil and somethin' to write on."

Jimmy Sykes got up and walked to the bar. He returned with a ball point and a blank bar tab. The deputy drew a crude map on the back and pointed with the pen.

"You take your boat over there in the late afternoon. Turn up this little creek that runs west of her land. Leave the boat right about here then cut through the woods. When you get there go in through the back door." He sat back in his chair and took another gulp of bourbon. "Now, here's exactly what you're gonna do."

The men piloted their skiff along a river that sliced through a prairie of salt marsh stretching towards the horizon. They steered into the creek and followed it towards high ground at the south end of Dolphin Island. Wellons ran the bow up on the bank, but several yards of pluff mud separated them from firm footing closer to the tree line. He tilted up the outboard as Sykes tossed out an anchor.

They stepped over the side and plodded through the muck, sinking six or eight inches with each step. It clutched at their feet and made sucking sounds as they struggled free of its grip. Once on solid ground they stopped to scrape off their shoes before starting into the trees.

Wellons was slim with straight, dark hair that hung past his shoulders. He wore camouflage pants and a sleeveless, denim shirt unbuttoned to mid-chest. He had not shaved in days, and he chewed on a toothpick that poked out of his lips.

Sykes sported long, brown sideburns. Shorts and a T-shirt exposed chubby arms and legs. His small eyes surveyed the area, darting in every direction.

"I still don't see why we have to do this in the daylight. What if somebody sees us?"

"That's why we're goin' through the goddamn woods, Jimmy, so won't nobody see us. Let's just get it done."

Overhead foliage filtered the sun, but nothing could temper the heat and humidity. Sweat covered their brows and stained their shirts. Clouds of mosquitoes swarmed as they tramped through the underbrush.

After fifteen minutes they neared their objective. A small, white shanty with faded blue windows and doors sat in a clearing at the side of a dirt road. Besides a few chickens clucking and scratching in the dust, there were no signs of life. The two men stepped over rusted barbed wire that once kept goats from wandering and crossed to a back entrance that was open but for a battered screened door. They removed their shoes and donned surgical gloves before creeping into the kitchen.

A cast-iron stove stood to the left. Its round, rusted flue climbed the wall before turning and exiting to the outside. The worn linoleum at their feet was clean, but the pattern had long since worn away. A porcelain sink and an icebox sat side-by-side on the opposite wall behind a chrome and Formica dinette. They listened, but no sound issued from the interior of the little house.

A doorway from the kitchen opened into a larger room with a fireplace where two braided rugs partially covered a floor of rough-sawn planking. A small TV with rabbit ears sat on a stand opposite a slip-covered sofa, and piles of books occupied one corner. The place smelled of age and charred wood.

Another door led to the bedroom. They could hear the hum of an electric fan and see the indistinct form of a small woman on the bed. An open book on her bosom rose and fell with her slow but regular breathing. Several framed photographs sat atop a chest of drawers. A comb, a hairbrush and a set of dentures were reflected in an ornate mirror that looked out of place in the tiny room.

Wellons unfolded a white trash bag, as his partner crept to the side of the bed. In one fluid motion Sykes grabbed the woman's wrists and pinned her legs with his body. Sally Timms woke instantly. She sat straight up. Her book fell to the floor, and her expression of surprise twisted into a mask of terror as the bag slipped over her head.

She thrashed but she was no match for Sykes. She screamed but the plastic trapped the sound, and a pillow forced her head back down on the bed. Sally's small frame shuddered as she struggled to inhale.

Sykes looked up at Wellons, "You think it hurts her?"

"Who knows? Just hold on."

Her contortions shook the bed, but soon they slowed and weakened and then stopped altogether. The two watched, hardly breathing themselves, before Sykes let go of her arms.

"Okay, it's over. Let's go."

"We gotta be sure. We'll wait a couple more minutes."

Sykes got to his feet. His hands were sweaty, and he fumbled in his pocket for a pack of Camels.

"You outa your mind?" Wellons asked. "She don't smoke. What do you think will happen when they find her and smell cigarettes?"

"I . . . I didn't think about that."

"You don't think about shit."

Pursing his lips around his toothpick, Wellons reached for the old woman's wrist. He felt no pulse. He waited a full minute and checked again.

"Okay, she's gone."

He removed the bag from Sally's head and closed her partially opened eyes. He folded her brown hands on her breast and replaced the pillow beneath her head.

Sykes picked up the book and set it on the chest, and after smoothing the bedcovers the two men left the way they had come.

It was not like Sally to miss a prayer meeting. Her friends were concerned. Immediately afterwards Lashawn Williams drove down the dirt road to Sally's place. No light could be seen through the windows. She mounted the three wooden steps to the porch and knocked. No answer. She opened the unlocked door and called. Again, no response. Lashawn switched on a floor lamp and forced herself to cross to the bedroom and peek inside. Enough light penetrated that she could see Sally's still form on the bed.

"Sally?" she called softly. "Sally? Sally?" she cried louder each time. Lashawn watched her friend's still body for a few seconds more and then, terrified, she bolted. "Oh Lawd, oh my Lawd!" She ran screaming out of the house.

She was still hyperventilating when she found Sam Green, who doubled as undertaker and coroner. He spent several minutes calming her before following her back to Sally's.

He made a cursory examination of the body.

"She dead fo' sho, still warm but dead. Musta' lie down fo' a nap and die in her sleep."

Sam found nothing suspicious about Sally's death. He found no open wounds, no contusions, and no broken bones, but he didn't notice the faint discoloration of the dark skin on her wrists. Nor did he lift her eyelids to search for tiny hemorrhages that might be signs of suffocation. Sam would never have guessed that Sally might have been murdered.

He unfolded a pale green bed sheet stenciled *Beaufort County* and draped it over her body. "Ain't no reason to pack her off to de mainland. I kin take care of it all. You jus' go on home."

Lashawn began to weep. Great whooping sobs burst from her lips, and the brim of her big hat flopped up and down as her body convulsed with grief.

The news of Sally's death devastated Twilight Pinckney. She had visited with her grandmother just a week earlier. They spent several hours together picking berries and baking a pie. When Cooper was a youngster, Twilight often brought him along. Sally delighted in the little white boy and made cookies especially for him.

When Twilight phoned Cooper at his office in Atlanta he could hear the grief in her voice. She had no other close family, and he knew she thought of him as her own. She had raised him after the accident when his own mother could not. He promised to make the five hour drive home after work. Tomorrow he would help with arrangements for the funeral.

Next morning they took a skiff to Dolphin Island where Sam Green met them at the dock. He explained how Lashawn found Sally in her bed, and he assured them that the old woman had died in her sleep.

"Wasn't no scratch on her. Ol' heart just wear out while she sleep in de bed. Nuttin' more to it."

Sam drove them to Sally's place in his pickup, and they all went inside. Twilight found nothing out of place in the front room. She looked all around the house, and everything appeared as it should. But when she entered the bedroom she noticed the book on the chest, and the bookmark she had made as a child on the nightstand. It featured tiny, multi-colored beads stitched in an Indian pattern on a strip of soft leather. Sally treasured it and kept it in whatever book she was reading.

Sam swore he had not touched the book. He hadn't even noticed it, and Lashawn had been too terrified even to enter the room.

Sally usually read herself to sleep. If she had put the book on the chest why was the bookmark not in it? If she had died in her sleep, as Sam said, who might have taken the book from her hands? The questions troubled Twilight, but there seemed to be no answers.

Sally's coffin bounced in the bed of a battered Toyota pickup leading a column of ancient sedans and golf carts along the root-strewn, dirt path to the cemetery. The procession meandered through a maritime forest of holly, cabbage palms, and saw palmettos struggling to soak up sunlight through the canopy of towering pines and live oaks. Bits of shrubbery snatched at the mourners, and a few held handkerchiefs to their faces to avoid inhaling the billowing dust. As the cortège neared the gate the smell of the sea hung heavy in the air.

Sam stepped out of the pickup and gestured to the pallbearers. Four men slid the pine box from the truck and raised it to their shoulders. They followed him to the grave and lowered their burden into the ground. Family and friends approached in small groups and formed a semicircle that opened to the river. The women's colorful outfits and equally conspicuous hats contrasted with the drab three-piece suits and porkpie hats worn by the men in spite of the rising temperature of the late morning.

The cemetery occupied the bank of a tidal river near its mergence with the sea. Sunlight glinted from ripples in the current and played in the moss hanging from the oaks. Pelicans wheeled and dived as shrimp boats trawled the waters in the distance. There was no breeze and not a sound other than the soughing of the surf on the beach around the point. Even the insects kept silent, and the shade of the trees did little to quell the heat. Fans that fluttered in the hands of some of the women provided little comfort.

Reverend Thomas Bryant broke the silence. "Let us bow our heads."

The assemblage joined him in reciting the Lord's Prayer before he nodded to the pallbearers.

"Please open the casket."

Two men reached down to lift the lid as the mourners crowded closer. Sally Timms' gnarled hands were folded across her favorite dress—the pink one she wore so often to church. A string of faux pearls hung around her neck, and a corsage of red tea roses graced her left shoulder. Someone had arranged her white hair in curls, and somehow she appeared smaller than she had in life.

Hard work and heartache had etched her features. Wrinkles creased her café-au-lait cheeks. But there had been happiness, too. Laugh lines radiated from the corners of her closed eyes. The little woman appeared to be seventy-five or eighty, but no one knew for sure. Birth dates were irrelevant to the descendants of slaves on the Sea Islands. Headstones, though uncommon, rarely disclosed more than names and dates of death. But Sally would be buried with her feet pointing east. When her spirit rose up to fly home it would already be facing Africa.

Reverend Bryant launched into his eulogy. "We all know how often Sally came here to honor one of us, and no one needs to be reminded of her kindness to her neighbors. We shall not forget how she cared for the oldest and weakest among us." He looked around the semi-circle at the perspiring faces, "And no one has a better record of attendance at Sunday services."

He intoned the words of the 23rd Psalm, "The Lord is my Shepherd; I shall not want. He maketh me to lie down in green pastures . . . "

Bryant, a big man with a gray beard that covered his wide face, held a handkerchief in his left hand to mop the sweat that glistened on his forehead. His nostrils quivered as he gestured with outstretched arms, and two of Sally's friends began to sob.

" . . . and I will dwell in the House of the Lord forever."

After a brief period of silence he nodded to Cora Mason, a large woman wearing a dress and hat of emerald green. She stepped forward, faced the assemblage, and glanced at the small figure in the coffin before filling her lungs. She extended her hands, palms up, and began to sing.

The words of *Amazing Grace* poured forth. Her voice towered in the otherwise silent space, and her elegant delivery evoked images of the hundreds of others whose days had ended here. Cora held the last note for several seconds before finishing and bowing her head.

The formal service had ended, but several women continued to weep. The mourners moved a few yards away as two men closed the coffin and filled the grave with earth. Twilight introduced her companion, Cooper Hamilton, the only white in attendance. One woman remarked, "He all growed up now. How ol' he is?"

Cooper answered, "I'm thirty-two."

A man spoke next. "This place ain't be de same widdout Sally. I sho gonna miss her devil crab."

Another woman said, "You ain't never say nuttin' 'cept it 'bout eatin'", but everyone agreed that Sally's recipe for the spicy delicacy was the best on the island.

Friends offered their condolences. Sally's death had come as a shock to them all. She had been spirited and energetic in spite of her age. She had lived her entire life on the riverfront acreage that her ancestors acquired during Reconstruction. Most considered it bottom land back then, infested with snakes and mosquitoes during the sweltering summers. For years it had little value. But the advent of insect control and air conditioning changed all that. Property that bordered water on the balmy Sea Islands had become very valuable, and developers and their lawyers soon found ways to wrest it from its owners.

When the workers finished, the assemblage returned to the grave. Family members and friends placed objects on the soft earth. Sally's hair brush and mirror, her reading glasses, and other personal items formed an oval. She would have no reason to come looking for her things. But in the months and years to come they would blow away, wash away or simply disappear. In the absence of a headstone nothing would remain to mark the grave. Even the raised mound would flatten to the level of the surrounding earth as if Sally had, indeed, flown away home.

CHAPTER TWO

Cooper Hamilton's lips trapped a pacifier as he tormented a stuffed toy in his playpen on the porch. He could hear the tractor and the sound of his mother's laughter nearby. He saw her sitting on his father's lap with her hands upon the steering wheel. He pulled on the ears of his teddy and watched as the machine meandered in circles before lurching and rolling over in a cloud of dust.

Understanding did not flicker in his eyes. He could not have known that his life would change from that moment on. He would never again suckle at his mother's breast or giggle as his father's strong arms tossed him in the air. All was quiet but for the din of insects until a new sound, a keening, began to echo between the house and the stand of corn in the field.

Cooper began to cry, and when neighbors arrived later he had cried himself to sleep. They found his mother curled up at the edge of the field, her small frame shuddering with now silent screams.

The doctors offered little hope. Ettie Hamilton had suffered a breakdown—something they called catatonia. She had been stricken mute and childlike after watching her husband suffer a horrible death. The young woman could not care for herself much less an infant. Under the circumstances her sister and brother-in-law took them in on Spanish Island. But the Parkers had little free time. Melanie worked as a nurse for the county, and Henry ran a commercial fishing enterprise. They would have to find someone to help with Ettie and her child.

Melanie spoke to Twilight Pinckney, a young neighbor who delivered the mail. The girl had the mornings free and accepted the offer. She eased into the routine at the Parker household, arriving early in the morning before Melanie left for work. She helped Ettie to bathe and to fix her hair while speaking in dialect. She spoke unblemished English as well, but she preferred the language of the island. Melanie understood and spoke some of it herself. Ettie paid little attention, but Twilight always seemed to know what she was thinking.

At twelve, Cooper was at home on the beach as much as the gulls and the ghost crabs. Like theirs, his days conformed to the tides. He patrolled the water's edge, scanning the sea and the sand stretching out before him.

On spring and summer nights loggerhead turtles lumbered ashore, heaving across the sand to lay eggs at the base of the dunes. He followed their tank-like tracks the next day and marked the nests with pieces of driftwood. He would watch weeks later when the hatchlings scrambled for the safety of the sea. As he approached the folly, a solitary pelican stood motionless, hoping to snatch a morsel sweeping by in the current. A broken wing hung at its side.

"It's okay, bird. I brought you something to eat."

Cooper pulled several bait fish from a paper bag and tossed them at the creature's feet. He watched as it snatched them up. He had stumbled upon it a few days earlier, and he knew it would soon die. He would feed it, he decided, until it died or fell victim to a fox or a bobcat. He could accept that. Twilight had told him about the cycle of life. She explained that all living things must die in order to make room for new generations.

"When it's our time," she said, "we go back to the one source of creation where all life is created. It's a natural fact."

He thought she made it sound logical and beautiful in a way.

From another pocket he produced a pad and a pencil. He sat cross-legged on the sand and began to sketch the old bird. His hand flew up and down the page as he drew the feathers and the legs. When he fleshed out the face and beak, a realistic image appeared. He cocked his head one way and the other and considered his work while making small adjustments. After another look, he seemed satisfied.

He muttered, "I hope it makes her smile."

He sat still, deep in thought, considering his mother's condition. He knew that a tractor had crushed his father and that she had seen it happen. The horror overwhelmed her, and her hair turned white in just weeks. But he did not know that she had held him as he vomited blood and gulped his last breath. No one told Cooper that they had found her in the field as she convulsed with silent spasms.

Twilight encouraged him to draw. He started with trees and boats, and later he focused on animals beginning with

Shakespeare, her pet raccoon. He began to carry a sketch pad wherever he went. Like a tourist with a camera, if something caught his eye he would capture it. They took long walks through the woods and once they saw a turkey strutting on the forest floor.

"Look, that old tom is missing a few tail feathers," she said. "He was probably fighting over a hen." She urged him to sketch it for his mother.

No matter where they started out, they came home through the sanctum. Like an island in a sea of flora, it was a clearing surrounded by ancient oaks dripping moss like spectral fingers reaching for the ground. Only small ferns would grow in the shallow soil that covered layers of oyster shells discarded by ancient Indians. During the equinoxes of March and September brilliant sunshine streamed down from overhead, flooding the space with sultry warmth. On moonlit nights the place became an oasis of light, holding off the surrounding gloom.

A shell mound in the northeast quadrant had settled to four feet above the forest floor. Its flat top resembled an altar. The place seemed peaceful, but even in the bright afternoon sun somewhat mysterious. It was here that Twilight taught Cooper about the Spirits of her ancestors. Her long fingers moved in expressive gestures as she described the *plat-eye*, a creature that could change forms at will and torment the focus of its wrath.

Most homes on the island had blue windows and doors because evil spirits are repelled by water. Twilight explained in singsong dialect, "Wit' de doors and windows painted blue, de spirits ain't come tru." She conjured up mental images of the world of haints and witches, and spun yarns that his young mind soaked up.

The beach shimmered in the early afternoon sun. Flights of pelicans floated over the tops of palmettos while black skimmers flitted inches above the receding waves. From overhead an osprey plummeted to the surface. With great effort it became airborne again, a mullet in its talons. Climbing and clutching its prize, it banked towards the nest where its young waited to feast.

Cooper got to his feet. Hands shielding his eyes, he looked out to sea. An offshore wind roiled the surface towards the horizon, and the tumbling seas made him think of a caravan of camels lumbering towards the south. Closer to shore he found the small, white spot that he knew to be *Swamp Fox*. Uncle Henry's shrimp boat was steering for the inlet. Looking over to the dunes he whistled and shouted, "Pooch, c'mon."

A black Labrador burst out of the sea oats. Together they headed up the beach. The dog was a beautiful specimen with a large head and clear, intelligent eyes. Muscles rippled under his coat. He came from a line of championship Labs bred by Wanda Odum, owner of *Dis'n'Dat*, the convenience store and café at the Landing. The puppy was her gift to Cooper on his tenth birthday. Cooper's pace quickened as he anticipated helping to sort the catch with Uncle Henry and Karl, his mate.

At Inlet Road he mounted his bike and started towards the Landing. Twilight came by in her Post Office jeep and pulled over. Pooch became animated. He jumped up and rested his paws on her window frame as his tail spun frantically.

"Good boy, good boy," she murmured scratching his ears and rubbing his coat. But when she looked into his eyes, he got down and sat motionless. His eyes never left her face.

"Hi, Honey. What's your Momma up to?"

"She started on a new doll after you left."

Only dolls seemed to capture Ettie's attention. Using photos as subjects, she spent hours sculpting their faces from clay. With an arsenal of tools from a manicure set she created life-like features. She crafted outfits from scraps of fabric and stuffed the forms with Spanish moss. The little figures were ringers for their real-life celebrity models. Her collection included big names from Hollywood, the sports world, and even politics, but she favored a pretty blond with a bright smile. Melanie dubbed her *Sunny*, but only Ettie knew her real identity.

"I'll go by and check on her when I'm finished with the mail, and you wash your hands before you eat anything. You hear me?"

"Yes ma'am."

Cooper rode off, but Pooch sat still as a stone until Twilight glanced at him again. Then, as if in response to a spoken command, he jumped up and bolted after his master. She ran her fingers through her long hair as she watched them go. Cooper had grown so fast. She thought back to the first time she had held him. Even then she knew he was special. She loved him, and she worried that he spent too much time by himself.

He didn't have any young friends, and he seemed content to spend his adolescence in the company of adults.

CHAPTER THREE

Cooper's sketch of the wild turkey won first place in the Thanksgiving art contest. At the end of the school play the Principal presented his ribbon. He could not wait to show it off at home. After early dismissal he ran towards his skiff, but three other boys blocked his way.

He slowed to a walk and pretended to ignore them, but Sonny Fletcher, the biggest, began to taunt him.

"You goin' home to play with your dolls?"

Cooper's mouth felt dry, and he licked his lips. He tried to step aside, but when the bigger boy launched a punch to his cheek, surprise and rage replaced the fear he had felt a moment earlier. He dropped his book bag and rushed at the bigger boy, but a teacher noticed the ruckus and interceded. He sent the boys on their separate ways. Cooper picked up his books and raced his skiff across the sound. He sped to the house and rushed inside. With a big smile he presented the ribbon to Twilight. She beamed and twirled him around the kitchen before giving him a hug. Then she handed it to Ettie.

"Baby, look what Cooper did? He won this ribbon. He did it for you."

The young woman's confused expression cloaked her feelings. She left the room and returned a minute later with her favorite doll. As always, *Sunny* wore a bright smile.

Twilight murmured to herself, "This boy is going places."

But her smile vanished when she noticed the red mark on his cheek. She brushed it with her fingers. "Child, what's going on? Have you been fighting?"

He averted his eyes, "No, ma'am, it's nothing."

Twilight persisted. She would not let up until she had the whole story, and when Melanie noticed Cooper's welt later, Twilight shared what she had learned.

Melanie said, "You know, the other day I heard another boy call him 'Doll Baby'. He's always fetching moss for the dolls, so I didn't pay much attention at the time."

Her face twisted into a look of concern as they exchanged a long glance, and Henry got wind of it before long.

"Coop, is someone pickin' on you at school?"

"Well, maybe a little bit sir."

"Son, what you're up against is bullies. Bullies is everywhere in the world and they're all the same. They're just a bunch of cowards that come together in a pack 'cause they ain't got the stomach to stand on their own."

"There's only one thing you need to know about a bully. If you stand up to him, he'll back off. If it happens again, pick out the biggest one and belt him smack in the nose. Then everyone else will see he ain't so tough. Remember what I told you about dog fights? It ain't the biggest dog that wins, it's the dog with the biggest fight inside him. You ain't nothin' but piss and vinegar, so I ain't worried about you."

Henry was never too tired to answer questions, or to tell a story. He taught his nephew to lead a dove with a double barrel .410, and to kill a deer with a .22. He celebrated when Cooper bagged his first deer. He rolled up his sleeves and helped to skin and dress the carcass, and carve it into portions to share with neighbors. He bragged about it later at the Landing.

"Cooper nailed 'im, bam, one shot clean through the head. That ol' buck musta dropped like a brick."

Two weeks after Thanksgiving the other boys confronted Cooper again. They ridiculed him as he made his way to his skiff.

"What a little jerk. All you do is paint pictures and play with dolls. Bet you wear a dress when you get home, don'tcha? You're crazy like your Momma. Everyone knows she ain't right."

At those words, Cooper stopped and turned to face them. Sonny sneered. "Your Momma's crazy, and so's that witch woman that wipes your ass. You ain't nuthin' but white trash. From now on you stay over on Spanish Island. We don't want you here."

One of the other boys had crept behind Cooper when Sonny pushed him backwards. He tumbled to the ground, and the two smaller boys pounced on him. He wriggled free, and as his tormentors watched his face clouded with a dark expression. He flew at Sonny, pummeling him with blows. The bigger boy fell to the ground with blood covering his face. Cooper pounced on him, jabbing with both fists, punching again and again until the other boys pulled him off. They watched warily as he rubbed his bruised hands and got to his feet. Sonny sobbed in the dirt as

Cooper picked up his books and walked off. He had never before felt the emotion that swept over him. He had wanted to kill the other boy. He would have kept hitting him until he was dead. The idea frightened him so much he began to cry as he made his way home.

The boy was growing fast. At fourteen his jeans barely reached his ankles, and his shirts felt tight across the shoulders. His easy smile and expressive eyes imparted good humor and intelligence. Most afternoons he pitched in around the Landing. He harvested a string of crab traps and tended to a number of chores. When school was out he would go along with Henry and Karl to trawl the near-shore waters for shrimp.

On summer mornings he wolfed down his breakfast before rushing to the Landing. His eyes darted from one to the other as he listened to the locals discuss the weather and complain about market prices, but because of his age he bore the brunt of many a practical joke. One day he watched from the dock as Ben Washington's boat tied up. Ben, a big, happy man, was popular with everyone. He saw Cooper and feigned surprise. "What dat I see over dere? It look like a boy, it move like a boy, but it got a face white like a marshmallow. How you dis fine day, Mr. Mallow?"

That drew a hoot from the others as Ben stepped from his boat and tousled the boy's hair. For weeks afterwards everyone called him "Marsh". He took it in good humor. He learned the ropes and carried his weight like an adult.

Cooper never tired of the trips to the shrimping grounds. He loved the big power plants that propelled his uncle's boats and the winches that retrieved the nets. With a cigarette dangling from his lips, Karl showed him how to change the fuel and oil filters and to check the coolant levels. Cooper's ears became attuned to the throb of the engines. He learned to listen for the knocks or vibrations that might spell trouble, and he discovered where Karl kept his stash of cold Budweiser.

At the helm he learned to sweep his eyes over the instruments every so often. Karl had mounted them so their needles pointed straight up under normal conditions. If one deviated from that position, Cooper would notice it right away. He would take it as a signal to shut the engine down until Karl could diagnose the problem.

He rejoiced when Uncle Henry asked him along on a four-day tuna trip. It would be his first venture offshore. He jumped up at four a.m., two hours before departure. Later, when *Blind Pig* reached deeper water, he marveled at the cobalt blue of the open ocean—so different from the greenish hues closer to the beach. He saw sea turtles basking in the sun and watched flying fish erupt from the depths, flitting fifty or so yards just inches above the waves.

At times acres of the surface would boil as legions of marauding mackerel attacked schools of bait. And just before noon, Henry pointed out a whale shark at least thirty feet long. Yellow spots and stripes splashed the length of its gray flanks. The creature passed by in slow motion, oblivious to the boat, as Cooper rushed to capture its image on his sketch pad.

He learned to watch for signs of fish—weed lines, oily slicks, or birds feeding on the surface. When no signs were apparent, Henry walked to the bow. He closed his eyes and tested the air, breathing deeply before exhaling. Disappointed, he returned to the helm to steer a few miles east. He struck out again, but on the third try he found what he wanted.

"Okay," he shouted. "Coop, come on up here. Close your eyes and breathe through your nose. Now tell me what you smell."

"I smell fish."

"That's right. We're downwind of them. They're coming right at us so let's get ready."

Henry shut down the engine while Cooper hurried aft to scoop chum over the side. As the gruel of ground bait dispersed in the water, it would attract the tuna to the boat. Karl dropped four lines over the side with hooks buried in chunks of mackerel. With the rods in their holders they waited, stepping lightly and speaking in whispers so as not to spook their quarry.

One of the rods suddenly bounced and bent, and in seconds all four lines were attached to powerful fish in the fifty to seventy pound range. Wrestling the critters to the boat involved back-breaking work, but as soon as one came aboard the line would go back over for another. The bite lasted twenty-five minutes but ended as abruptly as it had begun.

Cooper asked, "Why do they quit all at once?"

Henry shrugged, "Son, I been fishin' a long time now, but I don't know the answer. When the bite is on, it's on. When it's over, it's over 'til the next time."

They had three good bites the first afternoon, and by sundown they were spent. Henry deployed a sea anchor to keep drift to a minimum, and Karl fixed a supper of grilled tuna with hush puppies and coleslaw. When Henry wasn't watching he slipped Cooper a beer.

Later, with a full belly, Cooper climbed to the deck house roof. He reflected on the events of the day and listened for the song of a passing whale. He had almost nodded off when Henry appeared on the ladder behind him. "It's right pretty out here at night, ain't it?"

"Yes sir. Look there," Cooper pointed, "that's the Big Dipper. I've never seen it look so big, and right overhead that's the Milky Way. We learned about that in science class. That whole ribbon of light is nothing but billions of stars. I wonder if it could be heaven. I wonder if that's where it is."

"It just might be, son."

"I wonder if my Daddy's up there."

Henry didn't respond. He just patted his nephew on the shoulder.

"When I was little, Twilight told me that the spirits of all living things go to the same place. She said all new life comes from that very same place."

Henry fingered a cigar in his pocket but left it there.

"Well, I expect she's right about that. There ain't but one Almighty, and he created everything."

"Did you always want to be a fisherman?"

"I never give it much thought but I can't imagine workin' in some factory all my days, or livin' in a crowded city. How many people can sit out here and see a show like this? There's more to wealth than money. You got to remember that Coop."

"Yes sir."

"Let's go below and get some sleep. We got another long day tomorrow."

Karl had the first watch. The shipping lanes were nearby, and a sleepy helmsman on a freighter might ignore a small blip on the radar. The huge vessels could run right over a fishing boat. At one a.m. Henry relieved him and spent the time on the radio talking with other captains. Karl rose again at five while Henry caught another hour of sleep. Cooper's eyes popped open a short time later to the aroma of fresh coffee, bacon, eggs and grits wafting from the galley. He downed a generous portion before venturing out on deck.

He watched the darkness soften to the east as the sun sneaked up on the horizon. The colorless gray yielded to brilliant hues of pink and purple before the red-orange orb peeked above the surface. In just minutes it climbed into the sky to reign for another day.

Before the wind started nagging, the surface lay still. Bits of sargassum weed drifted by, and bubbles surfaced from somewhere below. Directly underneath at that moment, thousands, perhaps millions of creatures were swimming, feeding, and reproducing. Something about the vastness and the mystery of the sea struck a chord in his soul. He promised himself never to stray too far from its shores.

He felt the engine grunt to life and heard Uncle Henry's voice through the open hatch.

"Coop, pull in the sea anchor and then come on in and take the wheel while I get me some breakfast. I talked to Gilly Holton last night. He found a real good bite yesterday at the hundred fathom line. We'll try over there today. Keep her headed due east."

Three days later they tied up at the Landing in the midst of a commotion on the dock. Ben Washington, his wife, and his three children were all boarding his boat to go to Bluffton. Ben's aged uncle had died suddenly. Henry extended his condolences. He had known Acey Washington for years and bought crabs from him when the man could still run his own traps.

When Henry and Cooper stopped at Wanda's afterwards they learned the whole story. Acey had been getting by on social security, and by selling his hand-made crab traps to others. His needs were simple and he spent frugally, although he did treat himself to an occasional six pack of beer. His property fronted the May River and provided an unobstructed view of the pristine marsh on the other side. Most evenings he could be found in a rocker on his porch, sitting and watching the sparkling ribbon of water that had been his life.

One day a survey crew showed up and started marking off his property. Acey asked them to leave. When they refused the old man went back into his house and reappeared with a shotgun. He ordered them off his land. They left but returned soon with two sheriff's deputies who explained to Acey that his property had been sold by the court at a partition sale. He had no clue what they were talking about, but he didn't want to mix it up with the law. As he walked back to his house the older deputy followed him inside. Randy Heyward had grown up three blocks away. He put an arm around Acey's shoulder and explained as gently as he could that the house and property no longer belonged to him. It was heir's property. One of his relatives had petitioned the court to sell it, and the proceeds would be divided equally among all of them. Acey would get his share, but he would have to find somewhere else to live.

The old riverman slumped into an overstuffed chair and looked out the window. After a minute he stammered, "How long I got?"

Randy replied, "The law says you got thirty days. But if you run into a bind you let me know. I'll see if I can get you some more time."

The old man's watery eyes stared again at the river. He seemed not to be listening.

"Acey, did you understand what I said?"

The old man nodded.

Randy shook his head, "I sure am sorry about all this. If there is anything you need, you just call for me. Listen, I got to go now. Got another call. Remember Acey, you need anything, you just call the office and ask for Randy. I'll get back with you as soon as I can."

The deputy stepped outside and crossed the yard. He had made it halfway to his cruiser when he heard the blast. The sound of the shotgun thundered through the screen door, and dozens of egrets roosting in a nearby tree took to the air. Randy spun around, ducked and reached instinctively for his weapon before comprehension registered on his face.

"Aw, shit," is all he could say.

CHAPTER FOUR

The Grimes family had lived on the island for a year before Cooper really noticed Kathleen. Her father, Luther, fished for Uncle Henry and her mother worked as a housekeeper at a hotel on Hilton Head. When she wasn't in uniform she wore the dresses and bonnets of her Mennonite faith. Rachael Grimes, a tall, spare woman had desperation in her eyes, but Kathleen's expressed wonder and enthusiasm for life.

Cooper was a year ahead of her in school, but they often rode together in his skiff. Their mutual indifference yielded first to a platonic friendship and later to a more meaningful relationship. Neither had any other close friends and they began to spend their free time together.

During the summers Kathleen worked at *Sweets* on Hilton Head, scooping ice cream into cones. Cooper went shrimping with Uncle Henry and Karl, but in the evenings, with *Swamp Fox* back at the dock, they were usually together.

On their free days they walked the beach for hours, skipping sand dollars along the tops of waves. They watched dolphins surface just yards away and threw a ball for Pooch to retrieve. Sometimes Cooper brought along his .22. He taught Kathleen to shoot as Uncle Henry had taught him.

"Remember to keep both eyes open and squeeze, don't jerk."

After she learned the basics they had contests using driftwood or sea shells as targets. Kathleen sometimes won.

"I don't understand how you could kill anything, especially a deer," she said one day.

"We don't shoot them just for fun. We use the meat, and we share it. It's only wrong if you kill more than you can use."

"Well, I would never kill a deer. I would never shoot any living thing."

With her father out fishing and her mother at work across the sound, Kathleen had to fend for herself. Wanda adored her and intercepted her one afternoon.

"Hi, honey. Come on in and keep me company for a spell."

Wanda handed her a Coke from the cooler. Back home in Georgia Wanda had seen how an unplanned pregnancy could shatter a young girl's dreams.

"I want you to promise me something. I know you love Cooper, but you are both young. Tell me you will stay a virgin until the day you are married."

She fixed Kathleen with an unwavering gaze. "Will you make me that promise?"

Kathleen looked into her eyes and hugged her more tightly. "I promise you."

"Good girl, here." Wanda produced a dime from the cash register. "Go play H-12 on the juke box. It's a new group, a couple of sisters from up north. They're real good."

The strains of *I'll Hide My Love* by the Shortcuts filled the room as Wanda beamed at her young friend.

On the beach several weeks later Cooper's hand slipped between her legs. Kathleen stopped him. "I love you, Coop. I love you so much I hurt. I dream about you at night and I think about us doing it together, but we're not going to until we are married."

She leaned over and kissed his lips before placing his hand on her breast. "You can touch me here if you want," she whispered.

Kathleen became one of Cooper's favorite subjects. Her image adorned the walls of his room. One sketch captured the left side of her face as she sat on the beach looking out at the waves. It was a study in beauty and innocence. Another day, Cooper persuaded her to pose semi-nude and captured her sitting like a nymph in a fork of huge live oak. Only her torso and the side of her face were portrayed, but the image of her up-stretched neck and breasts made her appear as a goddess. He hid that particular rendering away in his closet.

In the year since Kathleen and Wanda had their talk Kathleen was true to her promise. The two youngsters were even more inseparable, but technically they were still virgins. They planned to marry, but when Cooper won a scholarship to College of Charleston they knew they would have to wait. He would enroll in just three short months.

School was out. Cooper went shrimping every day with Henry and Karl, and Kathleen was back at *Sweets*. Usually she finished in time to catch the last ferry, but when the boat left without her she would sit at the terminal and read. Later, Cooper would come for her in the skiff. She rarely waited more than an hour until the day *Swamp Fox* fouled a net.

Henry needed to know if the area being trawled had promise, but the frequent setting and retrieving of the main nets took too long. He deployed another smaller net that he pulled every half-hour or so. Called a "try net", the contents gave him a reliable estimate of the harvest of the larger nets. Based on the yield, he would decide whether to continue the trawl or to move on to a more productive spot.

On this particular day the device somehow drifted forward and twisted up in the propeller. Cooper had to go overboard and struggle for three hours to cut the tough cordage away. When they finally tied up at the Landing he was spent, but when he learned Kathleen had not yet come home he set out across the sound.

As he tied up at the ferry slip in the near dark he heard screams and saw four forms struggling on the ground. He jumped to the dock and sprinted to the scene. Kathleen was naked from the waist up, her skirt bunched up around her waist and her panties lay on the ground beside her. Two boys were holding her down, and the third, Sonny Fletcher, straddled her.

Sonny was blinded by his lust and didn't notice Cooper bearing down on him. The next instant he sat sprawled on the ground. A blow to his jaw literally lifted him from his haunches and rendered him temporarily senseless. Cooper turned and started after the other two boys, but they had a good head start. Turning back, he knelt by Kathleen and held her next to him. When he saw she was not badly hurt his fury refocused on Sonny. Cooper reached for his arm and jerked him to a sitting position.

"Get up," he commanded. "Get up you bastard." He leaned forward and slapped the fat face as hard as he could. When the bigger boy did not move, Cooper twisted his arm behind his back and forced him to his feet. Hearing something snap, he dropped the arm and stepped in front of him, launching a blow to his face.

Sonny fell to the ground, wailing, as Cooper turned away in disgust. The buttons were torn out of Kathleen's uniform blouse, and her bra had been ripped off. He wriggled out of his T-shirt and helped her on with it. It smelled of fish and sea water, but it covered her nakedness. With his arm around her shoulders he guided her to the skiff. As they rode silently across the sound he noticed the cold look in her eyes—not so much fear as something more sinister.

The next afternoon after *Swamp Fox* tied up at the Landing two uniformed deputies arrived in a sheriff's launch. They crossed the dock to the big shrimp boat.

One of them waved, "Hey Henry, you got a minute?"

"Hey Dave, what's up?" Henry smiled at David Grant, a fellow member of the VFW Post in Beaufort.

"Henry, I hate to have to tell you this, but we got to arrest Cooper. He's been charged with aggravated assault."

Henry's face contorted with anger. "What in hell are you talkin' about?"

"Don't get all riled up, Henry. We're just doin' our job."

"What do you mean doin' your job? Cooper ain't done nothin'. He didn't assault nobody. He's been out shrimpin' with me every day for the last week."

"Well last night he put another boy in the hospital with a broken jaw, a broken nose and a dislocated shoulder."

"Cooper, what's this all about?" Henry looked directly at his nephew and noticed for the first time that his knuckles were red and bruised. "What's goin' on?"

"After we got in last night I went to get Kathleen. When I got to the ferry slip Sonny Fletcher and two others had her on the ground. Her clothes were all torn and Sonny was on top of her. He . . ."

"Hold it right there, son," said his uncle. "Are you sayin' they meant to rape Kathleen?"

"Yes, sir."

"You hear that Dave? That Fletcher kid is nothing but trouble. He's the one you ought to arrest. Cooper was tryin' to protect that girl from those punks. That ain't no crime."

"That's the first I heard about any girl," Dave said. He looked at Cooper, "Why didn't she report it?"

"There was no one around. It was almost dark. She was scared and shook up, but I got there before anything really happened, I mean before they did anything real bad to her. I just took her home."

"Well the boy in the hospital has two witnesses, two other boys who say you attacked him for no reason. They didn't say nothin' about no girl being involved."

"They're lying," said Cooper. "They were holding her down."

"I'm sorry son. We just got to do our job. Henry, you can come over this evening and carry him home, but we got to take him to Beaufort and book him. And you might want to call a lawyer. The other kid's mother is the sister of some big shot in Columbia."

"You're damn right I'll call a lawyer. This ain't nothin' but a setup. Cooper, you go along and don't cause no trouble, but don't answer no questions until Billy Adams shows up. He'll get this straightened out in no time."

Dave Grant crossed the dock to Henry and put his hand on his shoulder. "Henry, you got my word we'll take good care of him."

"I know you will, Dave, but he's a good kid and this is so goddamn unfair."

Henry hobbled up the ramp towards his office. Wanda intercepted him. She had been watching the whole time.

"What's that all about?"

He told her what he knew and asked, "Have you seen Kathleen?"

Wanda shook her head before looking over her shoulder. "Here she comes now." The ferry had come into view. Henry continued to his office and dialed the number of his old friend and high school classmate, attorney Billy Adams.

It took less than five minutes for Wanda to pry the story from Kathleen. She worried, but Kathleen seemed to suffer no ill effects, physical or otherwise.

"You poor thing, you must have been scared half to death."

"I think more angry than scared. They had no right to touch me like that. If I'd had a gun I think I would have shot them."

"Oh, Honey, I'm so sorry. Did you tell your mother?"

Kathleen's eyes filled with tears. "No, I thought she would blame it on me."

Billy Adams' eyes were always open wide. They conveyed a look of perpetual surprise. A small, dapper man of five and a half feet, he wore freshly pressed suits and had a penchant for bow ties. But Billy was afflicted with stuttering. The more excited he became, the more he stuttered. When Henry arrived at the jail, Billy and Cooper were waiting for him. The two older men shook hands as they walked outside into the cool, evening air.

"Henry, this here is suh . . . somthin' else. It seems the Fletcher kid's mother is the sister of the top guy at S.L.E.D., you know, the State Law Enforcement Division. Well, I don't know if you remember, but a few years back the kuh . . . kid's father disappeared. Seems he'd been beating his wife and son for years. Neighbors said they heard gunshots one night and never saw Marvin Fletcher again. I wouldn't be a bit surprised if the kid shot him and the uncle helped to cover it up."

"Anyway, Connelly, that's the uncle, made a call to Sheriff Whitby, and the Sheriff is about to puh . . . piss his pants. The word is that nobody in the department better screw this one up. This case is going by the books all the way."

"That's fine by us. Let's start by gettin' Fletcher arrested for attempted rape."

"Henry, you're reading my mind, but first the girl has to press charges. Her name is Kathleen, am I right."

"Uh-huh, Kathleen Grimes. She's a sweet thing. She works over at the ice cream shop across the sound. Been there three years. She's a good student and never was a problem to nobody."

"Will she press charges?" Billy asked.

"Cooper, you answer that," said his uncle.

"Well, sure. I guess so, why wouldn't she?" he replied.

"Good," said Billy. "Have her here tomorrow, and I'll be with her when she files her complaint. Just call me in the mornin' and tell me what time to meet you."

CHAPTER FIVE

Twilight's soul harbored the saga of her people. It kept alive a glimmering of the march to the sea, the holding pens on Gorée Island, and the stinking holds of the ships on the middle passage. There were fading images of the whippings and rapes, of being herded by brutes onto snake and mosquito infested islands, and languishing for generations until their captors retreated, vanquished by malaria, and yellow fever, and the boll weevil.

There were gentler tableaux, as well; images of the soft surf caressing the sand, of a fiery sun sinking beneath the marsh to the west, of the unique beauty of her island, and of the white child she had come to cherish.

She inherited her mother's love for learning. But as much as she loved to read, she spent hours exploring her Island. She rejoiced in the musty smell of leaves on the forest floor and the shade of the great oaks on a hot summer's day.

She had an affinity for animals, and they had no fear of her. She could communicate with them, yet even she could not explain how. She would visit the marsh and sit on a fallen cypress watching long-legged herons stalk their prey. She felt at home with the critters in the swamps, and she delighted in the chorus of birds and insects that filled her days and nights with the music of life. But most of all she loved the beach where, she believed, even God comes to be alone.

She would sit in the sand with her knees pulled up gazing over the waves towards the land of her ancestors. In school she had watched movies of the Himalayas and the Amazon rain forest and the Gobi Desert. Life Magazine gave her glimpses of New York City and Paris and the stars of Hollywood. She saw photographs in National Geographic of Mt. Kilimanjaro and the African savannas teeming with wild creatures. But she had also noticed the pictures of half-naked, toothless women grinning child-like back at the camera. She could not imagine living anywhere but Spanish Island.

She was descended from slaves, but felt neither proud nor ashamed. Slavery was not invented in the new world. Human bondage had existed in Africa for generations before the first slave ship crossed the ocean. Arabs traded black captives to black kings and chiefs. They were prized chattels who were obedient and accustomed to servitude. But the huge requirements of the plantations in the new world overwhelmed the supply. The Arabs had to find new sources to meet the demand.

They learned to exploit old rivalries, pitting the ambitions of tribal leaders against each other. Proud chiefs and their kin were most vulnerable. Their disappearance would end age-old rivalries, and their land and possessions would be ripe for plunder. Entire extended families would vanish overnight. Twilight had descended from those families. Many in the Sea Islands could trace their roots to African nobility.

The slaves developed their own culture and spoke the Gullah dialect. Their lives were harsh, but predictable. After laboring all day they retreated to simple, tabby quarters built by their masters where they enjoyed a little socializing. But because of their isolation, the news they shared was mostly hearsay or innuendo. Word from the world outside would come only with the arrival of a new face from the mainland.

As darkness descended, their voices became hushed. Their belief in the spirit world had come with them over the sea. It sustained them, and the local version called root magic exerted a major influence in their lives.

Everyone knew someone who had died suddenly, or lost a baby, or broken a leg. Whispered tales of root doctors, witches, and haints passed from one generation to the next, and no one would pretend that he or she had not heard the message of far-away drums carried by the breeze on the darkest of nights. They were not to forget. They must never deny the Spirits. They were children of shadows.

In her dreams as a child Twilight heard their voices. "You belong here," they said. "Stay and care for your mother and the others that you love. You will heal the sick and comfort those who are troubled. You will also have the power to punish evildoers, but use it wisely or it will turn against you."

Her mother had practiced root magic, but she also embraced Christianity, and she could somehow reconcile the two concepts. She taught Twilight that daytime is the province of things we can see and touch and smell. The night belongs to the Spirits. At dawn and at dusk, the two worlds are in balance. Yvonne would never make an important decision at any other time, and no one was surprised when she named her daughter Twilight.

She introduced the girl to the beneficial roots and potions. There were others, of course that were used for more nefarious purposes. She refused to supply *Goofer Dust*, or *John the Conqueror*, or *Blue Root*. Only charlatans would traffic in such things.

Twilight's spirituality ran deeper than her mother's. She had faith in the power of suggestion, but she welcomed whatever assistance she could coax out of the Spirits. She used her gifts to heal. Yet in the back of her mind she knew that one day she would have to call on the black arts to save someone close to her heart. It frightened her because to play with the devil is to deal with the devil.

She lived alone, but she never felt lonely. Most of her contemporaries had long ago moved to Savannah or Atlanta where jobs were more plentiful, but Twilight would never leave Spanish Island. After cancer struck Yvonne, Twilight became her surrogate. As her mother declined, Twilight ministered to her and to neighbors who were sick or in pain. She counseled others who came to her with a variety of ills, both real and imagined.

Now she lived by herself in the small house on Eagle Point Road where she was born. The land bordered Spanish River between the Ashley property and the Bell tract, the site of a former plantation. Shakespeare, her raccoon, was usually perched on her shoulder, and she kept two goats and a few chickens in the fenced back yard that sloped down to the water. Like many others on the island, Twilight lived on heirs' property and did not have clear title to her land.

Her needs were simple, and she lived comfortably on her Post Office salary. The Parkers paid her for helping with Ettie and Cooper, but she would have done so without compensation. One day Melanie asked about her romantic interests.

"I know some boys from Savannah and Bluffton. They're nice but they're boring. Besides, all they want is sex. If you ask me, sex is over-rated."

"You just wait, Honey. When you're under the sheets with the right man you'll hear a symphony."

They shared a laugh. They had become sisters under the skin.

CHAPTER SIX

Alternate patches of drizzle and rain accompanied Cooper and his uncle all the way to Beaufort. Low clouds scudded southeasterly towards the horizon, and Cooper had a sense of foreboding as they crossed the long bridge over the Broad River.

They arrived just minutes before ten. The air conditioning system did not work well, and humidity blanketed the courtroom. Attorneys scurried to and fro between whispered conferences, mopping their brows with white handkerchiefs. Cooper and Henry found seats near the front of the room.

At twenty past ten the bailiff appeared. "All rise. The Circuit Court of Beaufort County is now in session, the Honorable Jackson Weber is presiding."

The Judge and the Clerk of Court entered from a door behind and to the left of the bench. They were followed by the Solicitor and a big, red-faced man who went directly to the table reserved for the prosecution. He sat at the end with his back to a side wall giving him an unobstructed view of the proceedings. He might have been mistaken for another lawyer except for the silver badge pinned to his suit.

"Please be seated," intoned the Bailiff.

As the Judge conferred privately with the Clerk and Solicitor over details of the calendar, many of the attorneys found opportunities to greet the big man and shake his hand. So did all of the deputies who were present. Notably, Billy Adams remained seated.

At ten forty-five the Bailiff announced the first case.

"People vs. Joshua Dillon. The charge is grand theft. Defendant will approach the bench."

A young public defender named Braxton Culley rose and escorted his black client through the wooden gate to the defense table. Joshua was sworn in. He looked to be seventeen or eighteen. The Solicitor rose from the prosecution table.

"How do you plead?" asked Judge Weber, already looking bored.

"Your Honor, we plead guilty with an explanation," replied Culley.

"Mister . . . ," the Judge paused and looked down at the paperwork in front of him. Finding the young attorney's name, he continued. "Mister Culley, Trooper McDaniel stopped your client for speeding at two a.m. on the morning of May twenty-second. During a routine search of his car, he found four brand new tires in the trunk that were taken the previous night from Sea Island Tire and Auto. They had tags bearing the store's name and the price, yet your client could produce no receipt. Please explain that to me."

"Your Honor, my client's brother works at the tire store and has for five years. Darren Dillon is a valued employee. Joshua needed new tires so his car could pass inspection. Darren agreed to lend him the tires until he was paid the following Friday. My client planned to give the money to his brother at that time. It would have been just another legitimate sale."

"Maybe his brother should be charged as well. What do you think would have happened if your client lost his paycheck, or if he decided he needed it for some other purpose? I'll tell you what would have happened. He and his brother would have reasoned that no one would miss just four out of all of the hundreds of tires at the store. This is a case of theft, pure and simple. Guilty as charged. Fifteen years."

Stunned silence swept the courtroom as most of the spectators and all of the defendants recoiled at the unusually severe sentence.

"But Your Honor," Culley squeaked. "This is my client's first offense."

"Well, he won't commit another for fifteen years. Next case."

Two more defendants had their day in court with much the same result. Judge Weber's foul disposition did not relent.

Then came Cooper's turn, and Billy Adams escorted him to the defense table.

The Clerk read the charge. "Your Honor, this is docket number BC 2701811, the charge is aggravated assault."

"How do you plead?" asked Judge Weber.

"Not guilty, Your Honor," replied Billy.

"Let me be sure I understand, Mister Adams, your client attacked another boy without provocation, in full view of two witnesses, breaking his jaw and his nose, and his plea is not guilty?"

"Your Honor, the Fletcher boy and tuh . . . two of his friends were in the process of attempting to rape a young girl when my client interceded. Had he not appeared when he did, they would have done so."

"Who is the girl that claims she was being raped?"

"She is still a minor, Your Honor. We respectfully request that her name be kept confidential."

"Very well. Has she reported the attack to the authorities?"

"Yes, Your Honor. I have a copy of the report right here." Billy handed it to the Bailiff who presented it to Judge Weber.

"Mr. Adams. This is dated two days after the incident. Why did the girl not report the alleged rape attempt immediately?"

"Your Honor, she lives on Spanish Island. The Sheriff's Department has no facilities there."

"But, Mister Adams, the alleged rape attempt took place on Hilton Head Island. There is a Sheriff's office there, and it is manned twenty four hours a day."

"That's correct Your Honor, but the attack took place near the ferry landing, three miles away, just before dark. Neither the girl nor Mister Hamilton had access to a vehicle. She just wanted to go home."

"Did the girl seek medical attention?" asked the judge.

"No sir, no need. She didn't think it went that far, but the rape attempt proves that Mister Hamilton did not attack Sonny Fletcher without provocation, and in fact, had justification for doing so."

"Did anyone besides the two other boys witness this alleged rape attempt?"

"No, Your Honor. There was no one else around."

At that point the judge's attention shifted to the back of the courtroom. Several people looked around but there were just a few spectators without seats by the back wall. One of them, a tall, black woman, stood with her hands together in front of her. She appeared to be holding something. Her eyes were riveted on the judge.

Judge Weber forced himself to focus on the issue at hand. "Mister Hamilton, the boy you attacked and two witnesses swear that you did so without provocation. You have one minor witness who claims otherwise. It's three against one, Mister Hamilton. I find you guilty as charged."

After taking a long drink from the water glass in front of him, the Judge exploded in a spasm of coughing. His face turned red as he gasped for air. He struggled to his feet and stood unsteadily behind the bench, choking and gagging as he stumbled through the door behind him.

The room was still except for the slight movement of the black woman leaving the courtroom. Once out the door she removed her thumbnail from the throat of a doll. It appeared to be the tiny figure of a man wearing a black robe.

After twenty minutes Judge Weber re-entered the courtroom apologizing to the assembly for his absence. His demeanor seemed to have softened.

"Now, where were we? Ah yes, Mister Hamilton. Under the circumstances I have no choice but to render a guilty verdict. However, I note that you have never before been in trouble with the law, so the court is prepared to be lenient. If you choose to enlist in one of the Armed Services for a period of not less than three years, I will impose no sentence. Perhaps the military will help you learn to control your temper."

The courtroom erupted in whispers until Judge Weber slammed down his gavel.

"Order. . . ! I will have order in my court. What say you, Mister Adams, does your client accept the court's terms?"

Billy cast a sideways glance at Cooper, and looked behind him at Uncle Henry. Both nodded their heads in the affirmative.

"Yes, your honor."

"Very well, have a copy of his enlistment papers delivered to the Clerk within thirty days."

With that, the red-faced man at the prosecutor's table got noisily to his feet and left. Billy started out of the courtroom, and Cooper turned to follow when he noticed Sonny Fletcher sitting with his mother several rows behind him. They glared as each silently promised the other there would be another time.

Once outside, Billy lit a cigarette. He inhaled deeply and released the smoke from his nostrils, removing his suit coat as he did.

"Goddamn Henry, thu . . . that was scary. That old son of a bitch gets crazier every time I see him. Shit. He gave that Dillon kid fifteen years for takin' a few tires. Juh . . . Jesus Christ. And then, he kept starin' at that wuh . . . woman in the back. When he gagged on the water I was kinda hoping he'd choke to death, but you know the old saying, 'you're better off with the devil you know'. Under the circumstances, I think we got the best deal we could."

"Who was that at the prosecution table?" asked Henry.

"The Flctcher kid's uncle, Buster Connelly. He's the one from S.L.E.D.

"Mr. Adams," Cooper asked, "who was the Judge staring at in the back."

"Just some black woman. I guess you couldn't see her from where you were standing. She locked eyes with him a couple of times."

"What did she look like?" Cooper persisted.

"Tall, nice-looking, in her early thirties I'd say, and she wore a post office uniform. She kept fussin' with somethin' in her hands. It looked like a doll."

Cooper and Henry exchanged a long glance.

The next week Henry and Cooper returned to Beaufort to meet with Sgt. Lyle Tucker, an Army recruiter. They learned that Cooper might qualify for the Army Security Agency. If he passed an aptitude test he could go to the Language School in California, and the credits would transfer to college after his hitch. After basic training he would be transferred to Ft. Devens in Massachusetts where he would be assigned to a language class.

"It's a sweet deal for kids who want to go on to college later," said Tucker. "What do you think?"

Henry said, "Lyle, let me and Cooper chew on this for a few days. We'll give you a call on Monday."

One week later Cooper enlisted in the U.S. Army. Predictably, he was sent to a basic training unit at Ft. Jackson in Columbia. It was close enough for an occasional weekend visit home, but the heat of the mid-state summer made for grueling training conditions. By the end of the eight weeks he had lost twelve pounds. When he arrived home for a two-week leave he cut a dashing figure in his Class A uniform, with a marksmanship medal dangling from his chest.

Their time together was blissful but as both knew, very fleeting. On Kathleen's free days she and Cooper spent hours at the beach plunging into the warm waves and clinging to each other at every chance.

In the late afternoons as the sun dropped low in the sky, they parted company with a kiss as each went home for supper. Later, they would meet at Wanda's and dance to the music on the deck until she shooed them home at closing—usually at nine on weekdays.

Suddenly, the time had come for Cooper to leave for Massachusetts. On the day of his departure they kissed goodbye, but as the ferry muscled into the current, tears welled in Kathleen's eyes. She had a premonition they would not be together again for a very long time.

CHAPTER SEVEN

Cooper spent two months at Ft. Devens before being assigned to a class in Russian.

Three days later he boarded a plane to California where he found himself a continent away from the marshes and maritime forests of the Lowcountry. He bunked in a barracks on a hillside overlooking the bay, within walking distance of downtown Monterey. He was bewildered by the unkempt, beaded, and long-haired young men and women in town. They were the antithesis of the sensibly dressed young people of coastal South Carolina.

He began to realize that a whole new world waited for him beyond the salty confines of Beaufort County. He marveled at the mountainous terrain of the central California coast—so unlike the marshes and maritime forests of Spanish Island.

He had trouble sleeping at first. The barking of sea lions in the harbor below and the sounds of wind whistling through rocky passes were new to his ears. But he adapted quickly. He settled in, and within a few days he had made friends with others in his Company.

His letters to Kathleen included descriptions of his new discoveries, and he promised to bring her to California after they were married. He no longer wrote daily, nor did she. A month later he learned that she and her family were leaving Spanish Island.

Her father, at her mother's urging, had decided to serve the Lord. He accepted a position as Assistant Pastor of an Anabaptist congregation in middle Georgia. Cooper knew that everyone would miss her, especially Wanda, but he did not hear from Kathleen again. He continued to write for six more weeks with no response. He assumed she had met someone new, and he stopped writing too. He was hurt and heartsick, but his busy routine kept him from dwelling on his loss.

The classes consumed his time eight hours a day, and each evening he had a several hours of homework. Like his classmates, he soon found himself forming his thoughts in Russian. At night he and his comrades became regulars at the bars on Cannery Row, or at the Mission Ranch in nearby Carmel. Home could not have been farther away.

He went to San Francisco once to visit museums and galleries, but usually he spent the weekends with his friends, visiting the beach by day and one of the regular hangouts at night. Six months flew by in a blur, and suddenly the course concluded. At graduation, when orders were posted on the Orderly Room bulletin board, Cooper and sixteen of his classmates learned they were assigned to Germany. After a night of celebration they packed their bags for a short leave at home.

Eleven months to the day after his enlistment, Cooper climbed out of a jeep after a five hour ride through northern Germany. His driver led the way as they mounted the steps to an imposing house on a wide residential boulevard that boasted many other large homes. Several olive-drab U.S. Army vehicles were parked on the apron between the street and the sidewalk.

"Here we are Hamilton, home sweet home."

They assigned him a room on the third floor that he would share with another man. He discovered that maid service was provided, and that meals were prepared by a local chef.

After stowing his gear he penned a quick letter to Twilight and asked her to share it with the others. He wrote about his ride through postcard-pretty towns and villages. He described the narrow, cobblestone streets, quaint houses, and shops as an artist would see them. But he kept it short. He wanted to explore his new surroundings.

The huge living room on the main floor boasted enough sofas and armchairs to provide ample seating for nightly showings of first-run American films. A bar and a small dance floor complete with a juke box occupied a smaller room on the same level. This would be home for the next two years.

He made his way to the dining room, one floor below, and took a seat at a table with four other men. They swapped information about home towns and mutual friends at the Language School as they feasted on *Wiener Schnitzel* with sauerkraut and roasted potatoes. A uniformed waitress served the tasty meal.

After dinner Cooper followed his new friends up to the bar. He was no stranger to beer, thanks to Karl, but his new comrades introduced him to cognac. Much later, when he mounted the stairs to his room, his head reeled.

The next morning he rode a small bus with eight other sleepy soldiers to a site at an abandoned airfield. It sat a mere hundred yards from the East/West German border, but razor-sharp concertina wire atop earthen berms would deter even the most determined intruders. An array of antennae of all descriptions poked at the sky, and several German shepherds patrolled the inner perimeter.

Inside an olive-drab Jamesway hut, linguists with earphones sat at a long console twisting the dials of radio receivers and recording intercepted transmissions. Across from them, Morse code operators typed endlessly as their brains decoded intercepted streams of dots and dashes and transmitted impulses to their fingertips. Columns of five-digit numbers marched down continuous sheets of paper rolling out of their machines. In a connecting hut, two voice transcribers huddled over tape recorders, playing and replaying intercepted and sometimes garbled voice transmissions before typing the text in Russian. There were no windows. One could not distinguish night from day. The scene was eerily surrealistic and silent.

In the evenings after seven local girls drifted in to watch the nightly movies. It allowed them to mingle with attractive young men and to catch a glimpse of the American lifestyle. If one could overlook the uniforms worn by the men just off duty and the accented English of the guests, the place had the atmosphere of a fraternity house.

Before the Army, Cooper had no close male friends. Here he belonged to a brotherhood of twenty-eight. Isolation from other American units, two-hundred odd miles to the south, further strengthened the bond. The camaraderie became pervasive. Soon he caroused with his new buddies several nights a week. He began to date a local girl, and he did not remain a virgin for long.

Like the other linguists, Cooper could soon speak passable German, and along with his high school French he could get along anywhere in Western Europe. With a schedule of six days on, and six days off, he and his friends had many opportunities to travel. He captured hundreds of images of the people he met and the places he visited, and his art became increasingly important to him.

During the short summers he and his friends spent much of their time at nearby beaches on the Baltic. People called it the

Riviera of northern Europe, although even in summer the water was frigid. The area attracted hundreds of young women from Denmark and Sweden. Most were blonde and blue-eyed and had very liberal attitudes towards sex.

Cooper had saved his money to buy a car, and with six months to go before returning home he took possession of a brand new Volkswagen "bug". His recent promotion to sergeant entitled him to ship it home at government expense. He had also squirreled away his leave time and had four weeks coming. During his last few months he traveled extensively, visiting many of the places he had so far missed. By the time he left for home, his portfolio bulged with his sketches.

The time passed quickly, and the boy who arrived two years earlier went home a young man. He had forged lasting friendships with some of the other men, and a few were as close as brothers. He enjoyed relationships with several girls, and he learned that women in general were attracted to him.

On the last leg of his homeward journey, thoughts of Kathleen crept into his consciousness. It was now almost three years since he had heard from her, or she from him. He wondered if she looked the same. He knew that she would now be twenty. She would certainly have other romantic interests. It would be unrealistic to think not, especially since she broke off the correspondence. His reverie ended with a jolt as the plane touched down at Savannah.

He rushed up the ramp and burst into the terminal looking about for familiar faces. Uncle Henry and Aunt Melanie had promised to be here. After a minute he spotted them in the concourse along with Twilight and his mother. He ran to them and embraced them all collectively, and then one at a time. Ettie looked at him quizzically for a minute before the expression on her face gave way to a smile. Cooper bent to kiss her cheek and saw that her white hair looked very stylish. Twilight had fixed it for the occasion. He noticed for the very first time that his mother was a beautiful woman.

His formal handshake with Uncle Henry gave way to a bear hug as each realized how much he had missed the other. Melanie playfully squeezed his middle and said she could see that he hadn't missed any meals. How true. He and his friends had eaten like kings, but he knew that German beer had contributed as much to his girth.

He turned to Twilight who looked exactly as he remembered. They embraced, squeezing each other tightly. Twilight chided him, "So, you finally decided to come back."

Cooper laughed and grabbed her hands, twirling her in circles until she almost fell. He hugged her again, and smiling brightly he said, "Let's go home".

On the ride to the ferry he answered one question after another. It occurred to him that the last two years of his life were very much a mystery to the ones who loved him most.

They wanted to know about the people he met and the places he visited. They listened intently as he described the house where he lived, and the beautiful cities of Lübeck and Hamburg where he spent much of his time. He told them about the beaches of Travemünde and Timmendorf, and the brief summers when the sun shone twenty hours a day. He produced photos of his friends and many of the places he had visited.

When they ran out of questions momentarily he asked, "What's new on Spanish Island?"

"Everything's pretty much the same," said Henry. "You knew that the Grimes left and went to Georgia. Karl's slowin' down some. He coughs all the time on account of those damn cigarettes, but he's still the best mechanic around. The damn import shrimp has drove the prices down so bad it don't hardly pay to go out, and *Swamp Fox* stays at the dock most of the time."

"Wanda can't wait to see you. She wanted to come but she had to get with some fellow from Texaco. She's sellin' more fuel now, and he wants her business. And let's see what else, oh yeah, you'll love this, Fletcher is a deputy sheriff."

"He joined the Marines about a year after you left, but he was home in six weeks. I heard he couldn't hack the physical training, and they washed him out. At any rate his big-shot uncle in Columbia leaned on the sheriff. Next thing you know he's got a uniform and a badge. Don't that beat all?"

"Cooper," asked Melanie, "are you still in touch with Kathleen?"

He suddenly felt uncomfortable. "No. I don't know what happened. She just stopped writing."

"That's too bad. She's such a sweet girl. Wanda keeps in touch with her. Last we heard she applied to a nursing school and needed a reference."

The welcome home party was lavish by Spanish Island standards. The aroma of Lowcountry boil floated in the air. Ben Washington had barbecued a pig, and his wife, Charisse, fixed up some "devil crab". There were pitchers of sweet tea at every table, and bottles of beer overflowed ice-filled galvanized tubs all around the deck. Virtually all of Spanish Island showed up along with friends from the surrounding area.

Cooper arrived promptly at 6:30 escorting his mother. She wore a new dress, and the tiara that he brought her from Austria topped her hairdo. Along with a round of applause, there were happy cries of "welcome home."

He seated his mother as Ben stood up and signaled for the crowd to settle down.

"I like to say a wud or two. Dis place ain't be de same widout dis boy. We all miss comin' home from fishin' widout seein' his smilin' face to greet us on de dock. Now he home and we all be glad. Welcome home Mr. Marsh Mallow."

Laughter exploded before Cooper stepped up to Ben and held up his hand for silence.

"That would be Sergeant Marsh Mallow."

"I be corrected, sir," said Ben.

Cooper and Ben embraced, and Wanda cranked up the juke box. The strains of *Fräulein* drifted in the sweet air. "I got that one just for you, Hon," she said.

Cooper spent the next few hours making the rounds with a cold beer in hand. He was reminded how many people besides Twilight, Wanda, and his immediate family meant so much to him. He had hardly thought about them over the past three years. Yet here he was, and it seemed as if he had never left.

People had to work the next day, so the party broke up before ten. The running lights of skiffs twinkled on the sound as guests from the other islands headed home. Cooper hadn't had a chance to thank Wanda, and he went inside to find her.

"Wan, you sure know how to throw a party. I really appreciate it."

"You just being here is thanks enough for me, Sweetic. We all missed you so much."

One of her dogs, a big male, sidled up to him and sniffed his knee.

"Who's this?" He bent over and scratched his ears. "He's a beauty."

"Yeah, that's Sammy. He's won so many ribbons I can't count 'em. I try to ignore him so he don't get the idea that he's better than everyone else."

Cooper laughed briefly but his expression saddened. "I got your letter about Pooch. He was my best buddy."

"You two was like Siamese twins—always together. I could never figure out which one was havin' the most fun. After you went off he'd come and look at me with those big brown eyes like he was askin' where you was. It broke my heart."

"Where is he buried, Wan? I'd kind of like to put up a little marker or something."

"Well, Cooper I ain't real sure how to tell you this . . . "

"Cooper," Uncle Henry had heard the question, "Let me answer that. Somebody killed him."

"Why would anyone do that?" Cooper stared at them.

Wanda ran her fingers through her hair, "Honey, one afternoon we had a real nice group out on the deck. They was dancin' and havin' a good old time. Well, here come those cronies of Sonny Fletcher, you know the ones, Craig Wellons and that other fool, Jimmy Sykes. Fletcher knows better than to come around here himself. I'd shoot his sorry ass, deputy sheriff or not."

She felt under the counter for her sawed off shotgun. Few had seen it, but even fewer did not know about it.

"Well anyway they was about half drunk and botherin' some of the girls, you know that kind of thing. I warned them before about feedin' the dogs, but when I come out on the deck Pooch was finishin' up Sykes' hamburger. "I told 'em to get up and get out, and not to come back."

Henry interjected, "The next day, Pooch just up and disappeared. Three days later Ben found the . . . well, found the remains. There wasn't no proof, and no witnesses. We couldn't do a thing."

"Henry, you say what you want, but don't try to tell me those boys didn't kill that dog."

"Wait a minute. What do you mean, remains?" asked Cooper.

"Honey, Ben Washington pulled up a crab trap and found his head. We never found the rest of him."

"Well how do you know it was Pooch?"

"Cooper," said his uncle, "the crabs didn't leave much but whoever done it ran his collar through his eye sockets so we'd know."

Cooper felt the heat rise in his cheeks. He knew Sonny Fletcher was behind it. He said nothing for a minute as the thought burned into his brain.

Henry noticed the dark cast in his eyes. "Cooper, it happened almost two years ago. There's nothin' we can do about it now. "Don't do nothin' dumb, and don't get crosswise with Fletcher. He's a mean one, especially now he's got a badge and a gun."

CHAPTER EIGHT

With two months to go until the fall semester, Cooper had to look for work. He took a skiff to the marina at *Ocean Dunes* and made the rounds. He knew his way around boats, and several captains jotted down his phone number.

It was the week of the annual bill fishing tournament. The crews of local boats were busy re-spooling reels and checking tackle. He spent a couple of hours swapping tales with those he knew. Before leaving he stopped at *Southern Cross*, the big sloop tied up at the entrance to the harbor. Cooper knew she belonged to Carlton Jenkins, the developer of *Ocean Dunes*. Her captain waved as he worked on a winch.

"Morning Cap, pretty day," said Cooper.

"Sure is. You doin' okay?"

"Just fine. I'm Cooper Hamilton from over on Spanish Island."

"Glad to know you. I'm Rick Barber," said the man leaning over the side to shake his hand.

"I just got out of the Army and I'm looking for work. I've got the summer before I start school in Charleston."

"You know anything about boats?"

"My uncle's Henry Parker. I've been fishing with him since I could walk."

"I kinda' guessed that when you mentioned Spanish Island. Know anything about sailing?"

"Well, I know a jib from a main or a spinnaker, and I know it's best to keep the water on the outside."

Barber laughed. "That it is."

Rick was a handsome man in his late thirties with sandy hair and an easy smile. Crows feet extended from the corners of his eyes, testimony to his years in the sun. He put down his tools and stepped to the dock.

"Could you use a cold beer?"

"Sure," Cooper responded.

He followed Rick to the *Flying Fish Café* where they found a table outside shaded by an umbrella emblazoned with *Cinzano* logos.

"It's gonna get hot this afternoon, but being on this end helps. We usually get the breeze right off the sound, but I'd hate to be tied up back there." He pointed to the interior of the marina. "They don't get much air at all."

"Hi, Ricky," gushed a young waitress as she wiped the table. "What can I bring you?"

"Hi, Sweet Pea. I want the coldest Corona you've got with a slice of lime. How about you, Cooper?"

"That sounds good."

"Jeannie, this is Cooper Hamilton. He just got out of the Army. Lives over on Spanish Island."

"Hi, pleased to meet you," she said smiling brightly, unable to cloak her interest. "I'll get your drinks right away."

Cooper looked after her as she disappeared through the door.

"If I looked at her the way you just did my wife would find out about it," Rick said. "She'd hunt me down and shoot me like a dog."

Cooper grinned. "Was I that obvious?"

They both laughed.

"Okay, Cooper, *Southern Cross* belongs to Carlton Jenkins. You know who he is, don't you?"

"Sure, he's behind *Ocean Dunes*."

"That's right. We use the boat to entertain prospective property owners. Most of them have plenty of money and expect to be treated accordingly. We take them out for a sail and fix them a few drinks. I guess that loosens up their purse strings. When we've got prospects aboard I like to have a mate. If it's just the old man and his family, I usually take them by myself."

"I've had a hell of a time finding a guy who can string more than three words together. Most of the locals are a waste of time, and the qualified guys aren't interested 'cause the job's just part time. You speak the king's English and you present yourself well. If you're interested, I'll give you a shot."

They both watched a sport fisherman tie up at the fuel dock. She hailed from Georgetown, a hundred and fifty miles up the coast. She was obviously here for the tournament. The crew of tanned young men in their twenties and thirties looked sharp in their light blue T-shirts bearing the boat's name, *Hot Rods*. Three of them jumped to the dock and secured the lines while the captain mounted the ramp to check in with the harbormaster. They looked around the marina expectantly. Excitement was building. By tomorrow evening the place would be full of boats and fishermen eager to compete for a cash prize that could amount to over a hundred thousand dollars. The boats' owners would be here and the cockpit parties would be in full swing. The perimeter of the marina would be crowded with onlookers, wannabes, and pretty young women.

Jeannie came back with the beers. "Can I get you anything else?"

"That's it for now, thanks."

"If you need anything, just holler," she said, smiling at Cooper.

Rick pulled the lime out of the neck of his Corona and bit into it, savoring the tart juice before taking a long swig of the ice-cold beer. He pushed the wedge back into the bottle and settled back into his seat. "Ooh, that's so good."

He looked at Cooper. "How about it, want to give it a try."

"Sure, but I'll need some coaching."

"Tell you what, why don't you come by tomorrow around two o'clock? There'll be some breeze by then and we'll run offshore a few miles so you can get the hang of it."

"That sounds great."

"One other thing Cooper, get yourself some khaki shorts and a pair of deck shoes. Before you leave today I'll give you a few shirts like this one. That's our uniform. And I probably don't need to say this, but we shave every day."

"No problem. I got used to that in the Army."

Rick definitely looked the part. His Ray Ban sunglasses rested on his chest secured by a band around his neck. His tan contrasted with the teal Lacoste shirt bearing the *Ocean Dunes* logo on the breast pocket. He could easily fill in for the models on the covers of men's sportswear catalogs.

The next day was another hot one, but when they cast off the sea breeze blew a steady twelve to fifteen knots. Rick powered *Southern Cross* out of the marina past three newly-arrived sport fishermen holding in the channel, waiting for space at the fuel dock. They went by *Mea Culpa* from Charleston, then *Sea Saw*, also from Charleston, and finally *Ecstasea* out of Edisto Beach.

Cooper looked back at the three boats. "I'd love to have one of those someday."

"Do you do a lot of fishing?"

"I did before the Army. I love being out in the deep blue. There's so much to see out there. Catching fish is just a bonus."

"I know what you mean. Not many people know what it's like being out there with nothing around but the sea. It gets in your blood."

"Well," Rick said, "later on, when we get back, the harbor will be jumping. I don't mean to scare you, but beer will be flowing like water and there'll be good looking girls all over the place. I'm married, so it won't bother me, but I'm just telling you for your own good."

"I'll try not to be too nervous."

They laughed. In the space of two days they had sized each other up and each liked what he saw in the other.

When they were clear of the channel, Rick steered southeast.

"Okay, let's go sailing. First we hoist the sails. Cooper, take this handle and put it in that winch." He pointed to a bright silver spool mounted on the mast. "Now, turn it. That'll raise the main."

As Cooper cranked, the crisp fabric climbed the mast and *Southern Cross* heeled to starboard as the sail filled with air.

"Okay, good. Now take the handle and raise the jib there. Rick pointed to another brightly polished winch. That's it. Good. Now, come on back here. First we kill the engine."

He touched a switch and the muted sound of the diesel rumbled to a stop.

"Now we're going to trim her out." Rick pointed the bow towards the Tybee Island lighthouse eight miles distant. He tightened up on the main and the jib, and *Southern Cross* responded like a race horse given its head. She heeled over more and began surging through the seas with a soul-satisfying swish. There was not another sound.

"Wow, this is neat," said Cooper.

"Pretty cool, huh? When we get out to South Beach we'll steer northeast, which means we'll come about. It's no big deal, but remember, always keep the passengers sitting under the boom. That way no one gets knocked into the wet."

A hundred yards short of Barrett Shoals, Rick announced, "Coming about." When he swung the wheel, the boat veered instantly to port.

"I always split the distance between that red marker and the beach. There's plenty of water under us here. In a few minutes we'll turn more to the east. We'll run out to the Port Royal Channel entrance and when we come back in we'll have the wind behind us. Should be a nice ride."

As the boat moved further offshore, Cooper realized how much he had missed being with Uncle Henry on his boats. He stood at the bow taking the salty air deep into his lungs. Returning to the helm, he grinned at Rick.

"Man, I love this," he said.

"Me too. So does Wendy. When we were first married we bought an old boat and worked on her nights and weekends for five years until she was good as new. We had saved our money and we quit our jobs to sail around the world. Boy, you talk about young and stupid."

"Well, what happened? How far did you get?"

"We worked our way down the Bahamas. Then we crossed over to Hispaniola. We needed water and supplies so we put in to Cap-Haitien. You've never seen poverty until you've seen Haiti. Most of the people were skin and bones. Little kids with swollen bellies were everywhere and the Ton Ton Macoute watched everything. They're the secret police that answer to Papa Doc Duvalier, but they're no better than gangsters.

I wanted to get out of there, but Wendy's into art. She wanted to hang around a day or two and check out the local galleries. Haitian art is unique—you can't find it anywhere else. Anyway, on our second night there six guys with guns boarded us. They wanted us to take them to Miami. Then the Ton Ton showed up and the shooting started. I got Wendy below and we stayed there until it stopped. Thank God, we were okay, but the six guys were killed. Four were floating in the water, and the bastards pumped more bullets into them just to be sure they were dead and left them to drift off. Then they arrested me for attempting to help them escape."

"They told Wendy they were taking me to Fort-Dimanche for trial. Nobody has ever come out of that place alive. They say you can hear screams coming out of there twenty-four hours a day."

"At any rate, they knew she would give up anything we had. She turned over sixteen thousand in cash, and they let me go."

"Jeez, what did you do then?"

"Well, we still had about five thousand they didn't know about, and we got the hell out of Haiti. But five grand wouldn't take us very far, so we headed home. Believe it or not, this was our first landfall in the States, and for once my timing was good. The boss needed a skipper for this baby." Rick patted the helm affectionately.

"Wow, that's incredible. What happened to your boat?"

"We live on her, bullet holes and all. She's back in the marina."

"What's her name," asked Cooper.

"*Second Chance*," Rick responded with a wry smile.

CHAPTER NINE

Working with Rick Barber turned out to be a dream job. The two men became fast friends, and Cooper had enough savvy to know his place. Carlton Jenkins came aboard frequently with customers and was impressed with Cooper's interaction with his guests. As a native he could answer questions about the area and its history. He was well-groomed and polite without being condescending, and according to Jenkins, a damn fine bartender to boot.

Cooper's language talents came into play one day when a group of Germans came aboard. They had visited the sales center and were interested in buying property, so they were invited for an afternoon sail. Five of the six could speak some English, but one of the women could not. At a point when her husband debated the finer points of sailing with Rick, she stood forward by herself, entranced by the beauty around her.

From nowhere, several dolphins appeared and played in the bow wave. Grabbing Cooper by his sleeve she pointed and asked, *"Schauen sie, schauen sie! Welche Art der Fische sind sie?*

He responded, *"Sie sind vier Delphine. Sie mögen in der Bogenwelle spielen."*

The woman watched in awe for another few seconds before she realized he had replied in German. *"OH- mein Gott, sprechen Sie Deutsch?"*

"Ja, wenig. Ich war in Lübeck für zwei Jahre," Cooper replied.

She bombarded him with questions. In minutes all the guests were aware of Cooper's ability, and Rick was relegated to sailing the boat. He smiled and thought to himself, "This kid is something else."

When word got back to Jenkins, he called the boat. "Rick, this young man is a real asset. I know you two are close, and I'm counting on you to keep him in the fold. See if you can put him on some sort of retainer so that when he's on holiday, or summer break he comes back to us. It would be a shame to lose him.

"Yes sir," Rick responded. He had already offered a more permanent arrangement, and Cooper had eagerly accepted.

"C.J., next time you come by the boat I've got something to show you."

"Well can't you just send it up to my office?"

"No sir. I think it would be best if I show it to you right here."

"Rick, is there some sort of problem?"

"No sir. No problem at all. When you see what I want to show you, you'll understand."

"Very well, Rick. I'll stop by in a day or two. Please give my best to your lovely Wendy."

"Yes sir. Thank you. See you soon."

A week earlier *Southern Cross* had booked a group of four on an afternoon cruise. Everything was ready when the sales office called to say the guests were playing golf. They would prefer an evening cruise. Mark Long, Director of Sales, called Rick himself. Jenkins treated Barber like the son he never had, and Long felt threatened by the relationship. He knew that Rick would be pissed off, and he delighted in breaking the news.

Rick and Cooper resigned themselves to a long day. But after scouring the boat for overlooked details, they still had a few hours to kill. Cooper walked forward and began to look at the harbor from different angles. He climbed the mast to about five feet when he ran out of footing.

"Hey Rick, have we got a bosun's chair?" he asked.

"Sure, why?"

"I'd like to see what the harbor looks like from up there, maybe sketch a picture. Do you mind?"

"No problem. It's right here, I'll help you with it."

In minutes, Cooper perched high above, close to the top of the mast. Sketch pad in hand, he began to capture the sights that would make the drawing unique. It would be hard even for the most casual observer to overlook the tranquility and beauty of this magical harbor.

"Okay, I got it," Cooper called down forty minutes later.

"You can just stay there until I'm finished my nap. I'm not the damn concierge."

"That's really funny. Wanna see me jump?"

"Don't pull that shit," said Rick, concerned that he might actually do it. "Give me a minute and I'll help you down."

Cooper's eyes drifted away from his rendering as he scanned the harbor. He glanced at the café and noticed Jeannie smiling and waving. She blew him a kiss. He returned the gesture, but something caught his eye at the table behind her—a big man in a uniform had watched the exchange. At first Cooper did not recognize him in the shade of the umbrella, but it was an older and heavier Sonny Fletcher. Their mutual hostility had not diminished. The two stared at each other until Rick called up from below and helped Cooper back down to the deck.

Finally the prospects arrived, and everything went according to plan. The guests were enchanted as intended, but it was after nine before *Southern Cross* tied up in her slip. The next day Rick discovered Cooper's sketch in the galley. He was struck by the unusual perspective and showed it to Wendy who ran the art gallery at the marina.

"Ricky, this is not kid stuff. This is good. Look at the depth. See the treatment of the clouds? Look how he handled these shadows. Don't kid me Ricky, who did this?"

"Honey, Cooper did it. I swear. He left it on board. He must have forgotten it."

"Gee, what can they teach *him* at art school?"

When Carlton Jenkins came aboard several days later, Rick asked him to sit facing the side of the marina that Cooper had sketched.

"Take a good look at this section of the harbor." Rick extended his arms, encompassing the harbor entrance and fuel dock, the café and some of the shops in the background. "Study it for a minute or two."

He said nothing while his employer surveyed the scene.

"Very well, what's the point, Rick?"

Rick handed him the sketch and watched the older man's eyes moved back and forth between the image on the pad and the physical reality.

"This is extraordinary, Rick. Who did this?"

"I thought you would like it. It seems our first mate has no end of talent."

"Cooper did this?" Jenkins asked incredulously.

"Yes sir."

The next morning Rick told Cooper the old man had been aboard and noticed the sketch he left behind.

"He wants to see you in his office after the cruise."

"What about?"

"He's got a crazy idea that you have some artistic ability jammed in with all the hormones. I tried to talk him out of it. I told him there's more talent in a bowl of rice crispies, but he wouldn't listen."

Cooper launched a punch to Rick's shoulder and they both laughed.

Later that afternoon, Cooper was seated across the desk from his employer.

"Cooper, I have gone out of my way to attract the best and brightest people to work alongside me at *Ocean Dunes*. In that regard I think I have done well. I can't remember how many times I have personally visited top-ranked schools in order to meet bright young people, but it has paid off."

"Yet every once in a while, I meet someone who has no Ivy League degree, or perhaps no higher learning at all, but measures up to the others on the strength of raw, native talent. People like that are diamonds in the rough, and I believe you are one of them."

He paused and punched a button on his phone. "Alice, would you please bring us some tea?"

A voice responded, "Yes sir. Right away."

Jenkins continued, "Rick showed me the sketch you did the other day. I was impressed. I've spent a great deal of money over the years to promote *Ocean Dunes*, and your sketch of the harbor is every bit as professional as anything that has ever been presented to me. I believe you have a wonderful future ahead of you. But, I am selfish. I want to be sure that when you finish at College of Charleston you'll come back to us and not be lured away by some other organization."

Alice appeared with a frosty pitcher of sweetened tea and poured a glass for each of them. "Thank you, Alice," Jenkins said.

Cooper shifted his position in his chair. He wondered if he was really hearing this.

Jenkins continued, "I am prepared to offer you part-time employment until you finish school. During the summer before your final year I would like you to intern in our marketing department. In the meantime I hope you will continue to work with Rick when you can. I know you two are friends, and it's a perfect opportunity for you to learn more about the kind of people who are interested in what we've got to sell."

"When you graduate I will arrange for you to work with our ad agency in Atlanta. It will be a comfort to me to have someone up there who knows *Ocean Dunes* as well as you do. How does that sound?"

Cooper did not know how to respond. He blurted "I don't know . . . I mean it all sounds too good to be true. I don't know how to thank you Mr. Jenkins."

"No thanks are necessary. You have shown yourself to be reliable and professional, and your talent speaks for itself. I was astonished when I learned of your fluency in German. Did you know that group bought four oceanfront homesites? They could not stop talking about the wonderful time they had on the boat."

CHAPTER TEN

The deputy sat in his darkened car as the two men slumped in the back seat behind him. The girl's blue Chevrolet sat just in front of them in the poorly-lighted employee lot. He checked his watch—five after ten. She would be along any time now.

After another minute he noticed movement out of the corner of his eye.

"Here she comes."

As Jeannie approached, Wellons and Sykes slipped unseen out of the far side of the black Crown Vic. They grabbed her as she reached for her car door. She managed one muffled scream before a hand clapped over her mouth. They gagged her with tape and pulled a mask over her eyes before dragging her to a patch of grass. A car started somewhere nearby, and she heard it maneuver close by. Bright light peeked through a corner of her blindfold.

Rough hands snatched at her clothes and left her naked from the waist down. One after the other, the two men raped her. They punched her when she resisted. Her attackers made sure that everything could be seen in the headlights.

As he watched, Fletcher rubbed his shoulder. This would have to do for now.

It was suddenly quiet. Jeannie lay sobbing on the ground, praying the men would leave. Wellons walked back to Fletcher's car.

"What next?" he asked.

"Tape her hands and ankles and knock her around some more. When the late shift gets off, somebody will find her."

After his meeting with Jenkins, Cooper ran back to the marina. He couldn't wait to share his good news, but Rick looked troubled.

"When did you last see Jeannie?"

"Jeannie? The other day from up there." Cooper pointed up the mast. "Why?"

"You haven't seen her since?" Rick asked.

"No, what's the matter?"

"She's in the hospital in Savannah. Someone beat and raped her. She has a broken nose and a fractured jaw.

Cooper's face was blank as he considered what his friend had said. Slowly, his teeth clenched and he spat, "That rotten son of a bitch."

"Who," asked Rick.

"Sonny Fletcher."

"You mean the deputy sheriff?"

"That's exactly who I mean."

"What does he have to do with Jeannie?"

Cooper proceeded to tell Rick about his history with Fletcher, including the attempted rape of Kathleen. "He's the reason I had to join the Army instead of going to college. The other day after I did the sketch Jeannie blew me a kiss from the *Flying Fish.* That's when I noticed the bastard sitting at a table right behind her. He watched the whole thing. We locked eyes for a few seconds before you helped me down. He must have thought she was my girl. He did it, Rick. I know he did it, or that he had it done."

The drive to Savannah took an hour. After parking the VW, Cooper entered the hospital at 6:45. He secured a visitor's pass and took the elevator to the third floor. Jeannie had a semi-private room, but the other bed was empty. He handed her a dozen roses and tried to hide his surprise at the ugly bruises on her face.

"Hi Jeannie, these are for you."

She forced a smile. She could barely open her mouth. "How did you know I was here?"

"Wendy heard about what happened and told Rick. He told me. How are you feeling?"

"I'll be okay, I guess."

"Do you have any idea who did this to you?"

"No. They grabbed me from behind, and they covered my eyes.

"They? How many were there?"

"Two, I think. It was really dark, and I think they were wearing ski masks. They raped me twice, and I thought it might be over, but then they started to beat me." She sobbed, "They just kept hitting me."

Tears rolled down her face. "Why did they have to hurt me after they got what they wanted?"

Cooper held her hand. He didn't mention that it was probably because of him. "Do you have any idea who they were? Can you describe them?"

"No, but they stank of cigarettes and beer."

"Did they say anything?" he asked.

"No. All I heard was grunting."

Cooper leaned over and kissed her forehead. "Jeannie, I'm so sorry. I just wish I had been there. Did you report it?"

"Well, a deputy showed up when the ambulance came. He asked me a lot of questions."

"Had you ever seen him before?"

"You mean the deputy?"

"Yeah, the one who asked the questions."

"He comes in for lunch once in a while. He's really heavy, so I recognized him right away. He kept asking about the details."

"Do you remember anything else about the ones who did it?"

"No, but there's just one thing, I might have imagined it, but when they put me into the ambulance I glanced back at him. It looked like he was smiling."

The next morning Rick and Cooper were aboard *Southern Cross* waiting for their guests. Cooper paced the deck and gnashed his teeth.

"Rick, I know he was behind it. I can't let the bastard get away with it."

"Cooper, you don't have any proof. Besides, who could you go to? The only one higher up is the sheriff himself, and he wouldn't believe you."

"There must be some way to nail the son of a bitch."

"Cooper, I'm your friend, and I'm telling you to drop it. You have no proof, no evidence, no nothing."

Rick stood facing him. He put his hands on Cooper's shoulders and looked into his eyes. "All you can do is make trouble for yourself. You have a golden opportunity, so don't screw it up. Just try to forget about this for the time being."

"How can I forget? Jeannie looked like a punching bag. It wasn't enough to rape her, they had to beat the shit out of her."

He could not shake the image of Jeannie lying on the hospital bed, her disheveled blond hair framing her once pretty face with its crooked nose, black eyes and puffy lips. "I know she's no angel, but she didn't deserve that."

"Cooper there is nothing you can do. Please, just try to forget about it. Okay, here they come. It's show time."

They welcomed the two couples aboard and Cooper acted as if nothing had happened. He graciously attended to the passengers but Rick could not help but notice the fury in his eyes.

CHAPTER ELEVEN

With the credits from the Language School, Cooper earned his degree at College of Charleston in just three years. During that time he refined his style. His artwork became more fearless and sophisticated. He experimented with new techniques and took advantage of many opportunities to meet and mingle with his professors and guest lecturers. In spite of his heavy course load, he came home most weekends. When he did not crew with Rick on *Southern Cross* he helped Uncle Henry. Just being on the water buoyed his soul.

Carlton Jenkins had kept his word. The previous summer Cooper worked in the marketing department. It was great experience that would serve him well. And now, a month before graduation, he was off to Atlanta to interview with Dixon & Mayfield, the advertising agency for *Ocean Dunes*.

Atlanta is a magical place in the springtime. Dogwoods and azaleas sprout from every patch of unpaved ground. The fragrance of budding magnolias and honeysuckles fills the air as pretty girls pour out of buildings along Peachtree Street at noon for an hour in the sun.

The city had a pulse. It had morphed from a matronly dowager of the old south to a vibrant symbol of the economic expansion of the region. Cooper could feel its exuberance.

He parked downtown before noon but still had two hours to kill before his scheduled appointment. He decided to explore. As he mingled with the crowd he marveled at new and architecturally interesting buildings, including some still under construction. Atlanta's energy pulsated all around him, but it was very different from the staid but beautiful cities of Europe, and many millennia removed from Spanish Island. The idea occurred to him that he might grow to love this city. He could prosper with it.

The interview was not exactly what he expected. At two o'clock sharp a secretary ushered him into the office of Gwen Easterly, the Creative Director, and a well-proportioned, attractive redhead in her early thirties. She made no effort to cloak her physical attributes, nor did she seem to care if anyone noticed them. She had confidence in her importance to the agency, and she didn't hide that either.

Gwen knew that Carlton Jenkins had referred Cooper. No one had to draw her a picture. This was a rubber stamp situation. If her stamp ran out of ink she'd better have a damn good reason why. This kid couldn't be any worse than some of the others she had hired. She would go with the flow.

They began with small talk. Cooper described his experiences growing up on Spanish Island, and later in Germany. Gwen grew up a farmer's daughter in Virginia, and when she graduated the University of North Carolina she hired on with a small agency in Raleigh. The clients were mostly agricultural—makers of farm implements, hog feed and herbicides.

"You can imagine how exciting that was," she said before launching into the usual absurdities about how the glamorous world of advertising isn't all it's cracked up to be. She recited the caveats about long hours and unreasonable clients, but he didn't seem deterred.

She lit a cigarette, slipped off her shoes, and propped her panty-hosed feet on her desk. She looked directly at him and said, "I'd like to know more about the inner Cooper Hamilton. Do you mind?"

"Well, no. I guess that's why I'm here."

Blowing a ring of smoke towards the ceiling she asked, "What do you think would happen if the depth of the oceans suddenly dropped by two feet?"

At an advertising agency the creative team, be they copywriters or artists, are paid to come up with fresh ideas. The answers to questions like this gave her a peek into the thought processes of the person sitting on the other side of her desk. Expecting a series of "what's," or "what do you mean's," Gwen was unprepared for Cooper's answer.

"Well," he began, riveting her eyes, "that could be a real problem. For one thing, the earth might spin out of orbit because of the loss of so much mass. The ice caps could break free and drift closer to the equator, disrupting shipping at a minimum. Port cities might wind up being miles from navigable waterways, and our wetlands would be drained. The impact on sea life and seafood would be enormous."

He shifted position in his chair. "Our climate is regulated by the sea, so the loss of that much water would have a dramatic effect on weather patterns. We might get unprecedented droughts or, conversely, we might have more numerous and more violent natural disasters like hurricanes. Two thirds of the world's population would eventually starve, and the survivors would be hard pressed to survive."

"At the very least, the economy of the Western world would be in ruins."

Gwen slid her feet off her desk and squashed out her cigarette. This self-assured puppy had taken her bait and had risen to the occasion.

"That was an interesting answer. May I see your portfolio," she asked.

Cooper opened his black leather presentation case and proceeded to offer his works arranged in chronological order. First he showed her the black and white studies of wildlife and beach scenes on Spanish Island. Naturally he included the sketch of the marina at *Ocean Dunes* that had adorned several promotional mailings. She liked it. He hadn't copied anyone's style.

Next there were renderings of church spires, castles in Spain, and interesting architectural landmarks from all over Western Europe. One striking image showed Mont-Saint-Michel as seen from below on the vast tidal flats. Another dramatic piece depicted the American Cemetery at Colleville-sur-Mer. Regiments of head stones marched towards a battle-torn Stars and Stripes rising above the horizon in the background.

"Were you really there?" Gwen asked, impressed.

"Yes. I'll never forget it. It overlooks Omaha Beach. There were just so many graves, row after row of them, and the bluffs those guys had to scale to get up there were huge."

Sketches of pretty girls in swimwear on Baltic beaches proved that his talent was not confined to landscapes and buildings. He had captured distinctly interesting faces ranging from children to the very old. She loved one sketch that focused on the images of three aging patrons at a *Gasthuus*. They were drinking beer and listening to an accordionist. One could tell from their expressions that the tune he played brought back memories of happier days.

She wouldn't need her rubber stamp for this kid. They would be lucky to have him.

"Nice work, very well done. You must have enjoyed your time in Europe. By the way, Matt Dixon asked that I bring you by his office after our chat. I'll show you the way."

At the end of the hall, Gwen shook his hand and turned him over to Dixon's secretary. She thanked him for coming, and asked him to call at the beginning of the week. She would need a few days to review the other applications. He thanked her for her time as she turned and walked back down the hall.

She thought to herself, "What bullshit?" He had the job even if he couldn't spell his name. But she had seen his work, and from his answers to her questions she knew he was intelligent. She knew, also, that he would make a great impression with Matt Dixon. Her early warning system, in standby mode, chirped softly.

CHAPTER TWELVE

The new campaign for *Ocean Dunes* had barely launched when the trade press smelled a story. Both *Advertising Age* and *Adweek* wanted interviews with the creative team and a columnist for the *New York Times* asked for background information. It departed from anything the resort development industry had ever done before. The magazine ads pictured ordinary people doing ordinary things—driving tee shots into the water, or being knocked down by waves at the beach. In the background could be seen the amenities of *Ocean Dunes* set amidst the natural beauty of the property. The tag line read, "If only we were perfect, too."

TV commercials conveyed the same message but they were better able to showcase the beauty of the island. The director chose the talent carefully, and the photographer spent hours capturing just the right expressions on the models' faces. The copy extolled the environmentally-friendly development that became the *Ocean Dunes* hallmark with the slogan, "Visit the Dunes—for a day or forever."

People identified with the hapless characters in the ads. Word of mouth, the most effective of all marketing tools, began spontaneously, and Gwen and Cooper became minor celebrities in the world of advertising. They were guests on talk shows in Atlanta, and WTOC, the CBS affiliate in Savannah, interviewed them for a spot on the nightly news.

Dixon & Mayfield, or D&M as the trade knew it, had become one of the hottest agencies in town. They had revamped the creative approach for Jenkins' eco-friendly projects and branded his imaginative style of real estate development. The campaign attracted the attention of conservation groups, and Jenkins and *Ocean Dunes* were featured in articles in a number of national publications. D&M, itself, won a *Clio* for the state-of-the-art series of TV spots.

As Jenkins' empire blossomed, D&M's reputation soared. The agency soon had its pick of well-financed development projects up and down the east coast and the Caribbean basin.

Gwen and Cooper were a brilliant team. They were involved with all aspects of the campaigns they created, from visuals to copy. They were together, more often than not, at lunches, client meetings, and new business presentations. They traveled together to visit accounts in South Florida and St. Thomas and eventually they slept together, but no romance was involved. One night in Miami they returned to their hotel after a business dinner. They were both a little drunk and both a little lonely. In the elevator, Gwen grabbed Cooper's tie and pulled him close.

"I think I'd like to screw."

They had each considered the idea in the past, but neither had given it voice. All of a sudden the difference of eight years in their ages seemed irrelevant.

When the door opened at her floor she pulled him out by his arm and led him to her room. She was horny as hell. She undressed him first before dropping her clothes on the floor next to the bed. There was no foreplay. She hurried to climax and he marveled at the intensity of her lovemaking. Afterwards they lay spent, neither speaking for several minutes.

"I've got some scotch," she said. "Want some?"

"Sure." Cooper puffed up a pillow behind his head and watched her fix the drinks. She made no attempt to cover her nakedness. Her red hair framed her striking facial features—blue eyes and full lips—and her skin was perfect, not mottled and freckled like many other redheads. She was nearly as tall as Cooper. In fact, in heels she stood an inch or so taller. Her long legs were perfectly proportioned and her breasts were full and flawless.

She returned to the bed with the drinks. "I've thought about us doing that for quite a while. But don't get me wrong. I've got my life and you have yours. I happen to like sex. I like it a lot, and I like it with different men. It doesn't have anything to do personally between you and me. Besides, aren't you seeing someone on a regular basis?"

"You mean Mary Sue?"

"That's the one. Mary Sue Nordlund, isn't it?"

"Yup. Her dad is the real estate guy."

"Wow. There's some big bucks there, Coopie."

She had started calling him that soon after he joined the agency. At first it bothered him, but soon he realized it was just Gwen.

"So I've been told. But that doesn't have anything to do with it."

"I know you mean that, but don't be so fucking naïve. Money can't hurt you."

She put down her drink and moved to his side of the bed. Her hand slid between his legs as she began to kiss his nipples, but this time she did not hurry. As his fingers found her wetness she moaned and writhed to his touch. When she could wait no longer she pushed him on his back and mounted him, gyrating slowly at first, and then frantically until they climaxed together. They coupled twice more, experimenting with new positions, before falling to sleep, exhausted.

Cooper returned to his room at 7:30 before Gwen was awake. They had agreed to meet for breakfast.

At nine sharp the maitre d' greeted him at the door to the dining room. "Just one sir?" he asked.

"No, I'm meeting . . . oh, there she is." Gwen waved from a table next to the window. She looked fresh as a flower but dangerous in her all-business attire.

"Coopie, I don't know if these guys can cut it or not. They're new and they have some impressive credits, but do they have the *hunger*, that's the question."

She referred to *Gomez and the Gang*, the production company they would interview that morning.

"Here's the deal. We'll listen to everything they say, and we'll show them the *Ocean Dunes* tape. We'll ask how they would do it differently, and then we'll sit back, shut up and see what happens. Okay?"

"Sure. But why are we testing them on a property they've never seen?"

"That's just it. If they can show us some glitz about a project they know nothing about, what do you suppose they could do for one in their own back yard, like *Coral Beach*?"

"Okay, but isn't that a little devious?"

"Oh, Cooper, grow up for Christ sake. This is the big, bad world."

The meeting went better than expected and they caught the four o'clock flight home to Atlanta. Gwen loved the ideas presented by Hector Gomez and his associates. The concept of their original *Ocean Dunes* TV commercials was fine, but the background shots behind the humorous mishaps would emerge from a mist while the models' images faded and disappeared.

They would have more of the precious thirty seconds to showcase the beauty of the property.

Matt Dixon loved it. Carlton Jenkins loved it. It was a go. A new series of ads launched barely six months after the originals. If anything, the treatment made the mishaps more memorable. The new commercials depicted a man falling off a dock while crabbing with his son, and a woman's sun hat blowing off and landing on an alligator's head. They were so cleverly directed and so widely viewed that they became fodder for Saturday Night Live.

There was more trade buzz, more accolades for D&M, and more sales for *Ocean Dunes*. Gwen and Cooper had arrived. Strangers would greet them by name when they were at lunch, or having drinks at one of Atlanta's popular watering holes.

Just a few months later Donald Mayfield announced his plans to retire. He co-founded the agency, but he had become just a figurehead. He rarely spent more than two or three mornings a week in the office. Following his doctor's advice, he and his wife were planning a move to Arizona.

The man offered to sell his shares to Gwen and Cooper. It was a great opportunity, and with Matt Dixon's blessings they accepted. The three would be partners. That afternoon the pair visited Trust Company Bank to arrange for the necessary financing. They spent several hours with a senior vice president who assured them that their applications would be approved. After leaving his office they were off to *Dante's Down the Hatch*, where they both got quite drunk.

The two continued their occasional trysts more out of opportunity than design. They had learned to use each other sexually in order to derive more pleasure than they could from other partners. Cooper knew he was just one of many and wondered if he was being graded. But he knew deep down that Gwen hungered for him as he did for her. They were able to slake each other's lust without the baggage of love or relationship. It was getting laid, pure and simple, sometimes kinky but always exhausting and totally satisfying.

Once they did it late at night on the edge of her desk after rushing to meet a closing deadline for *Southern Living*. He took the initiative, hiked up her skirt and pulled her pantyhose to her ankles. With her legs askew he plunged into her. He had never seen her so excited. She moaned so loudly he was afraid the watchman would hear and was relieved when she climaxed quickly.

"Christ, Coopie. You really got to me that time."

"Anything for you, Boss Lady."

Cooper and his fiancée were lovers, of course, but Mary Sue could not lose herself to passion like Gwen. She would become excited immediately and climax quickly, lying back on the pillows and remarking how nice it was. But her very next words might have to do with an outfit she admired at Nieman Marcus.

She had a trim figure, natural blond hair, and the kind of face that demands a second look. They had met at *Timothy John's*, and dated for a month before becoming intimate. Afterwards Cooper stayed at her place as much as his own. He had spent six years as a bachelor in Atlanta, a city considered to be a single man's paradise, but he wanted to settle down. Mary Sue seemed to him to be the perfect choice. She had beauty, a quirky sense of humor, and they shared many interests. Both loved Chinese food, and they enjoyed first run movies and trips to the many museums around the city. It seemed a perfect match. When they decided to marry he was thirty-one. Mary Sue had just turned twenty-eight.

Her parents accepted him only reluctantly. His family and background were suspect, but his net worth and his status as a rising star in one of the city's top advertising agencies made up for it. Eric Nordlund even entertained fantasies about employing Dixon & Mayfield at a discount rate.

The couple bought a small three bedroom home on West Paces Ferry, and Mary Sue spent three months and many thousands of dollars furnishing it with the help of an interior designer.

CHAPTER THIRTEEN

They were married. In June at First Presbyterian Church on Peachtree Street. The bride's side of the church overflowed, but Cooper's family and guests took up just five rows.

Ettie sat in the front pew with Sunny tucked under her arm. Melanie and Twilight took seats on either side of her with Wanda on one end. Karl had stayed home to tend to business. The agency people occupied most of the next three rows and some of Cooper's Atlanta friends filled in behind them.

The pews on the bride's side were alive with whispers. Guests traded hearsay about Ettie, or commented on Melanie's outfit and the outlandish hat that Wanda wore. Uncle Henry was best man, and Matt Dixon, Rick Barber and two Army friends served as groom's men.

The ceremony at the church took only half an hour, but the reception at the Cherokee Town Club went on for hours. Cooper's family seemed painfully out of place. Mary Sue and her mother made only a feeble attempt to make them feel welcome before ignoring them for the rest of the evening.

Their discomfort was so apparent that Gwen left her place at the D&M table to join them. As a country girl herself she delighted in their stories about Spanish Island and Cooper's exploits as a boy. Twilight taught her a few expressions in dialect and intrigued her with stories about root magic.

Gwen learned about the fearsome *boo hàg* who slips out of her skin to become invisible. She would then appear in a person's bedroom and steal his breath away. To keep her out of the house people would leave a colander on the front porch. The *hag* would be compelled to stop and count every tiny hole, but she would lose count every time. That would keep her occupied until dawn when she would have to fly away. Gwen enjoyed herself, and even coaxed Uncle Henry onto the dance floor, although the limp he brought home from Korea made things difficult.

Before the band's last number Cooper asked her to dance. "Gwen, thanks very much for looking after my family. They're out of their league."

"No problem, Coopie, but your bride and her mother are lowlifes. I can't believe they left your folks adrift like that. They're living proof that money and class don't necessarily go together."

As the reception ended, the newlyweds sped away in a limo to a downtown hotel. They were booked on an early morning flight to the British West Indies where they would spend two weeks at *Reagan's Reef*, an upscale yacht club cum resort, and a recent addition to the D&M stable of clients.

On the island there were no meetings, no luncheon appointments, and no Junior League benefits. The place boasted a spa, but even Mary Sue could not justify spending more than two hours a day having her nails done and redone. For once they had the time to talk, to sit on the beach, and take long walks. But by the end of the first week they had little to talk about. The fact registered with them both but remained unspoken.

By the second week they pursued their different interests on their own. Mary Sue planted herself on the beach and devoured one paperback after another, while Cooper rented a jeep and explored the island. His sketch pad came with him as he captured landscapes and seascapes, but the natives did not escape his attention. The buoyant images that resulted from his intrusion on their private moments would make a collection of their own. Several would be woven into the ads and commercials for *Reagan's Reef*.

The couple regrouped for cocktails at the end of the day and returned to one of the three island restaurants for dinner. With four days to go they couldn't wait to leave. Cooper ascribed their mutual disaffection to the slow pace and the isolation of the tiny island. He felt sure things would return to normal once they were home.

His spirits lifted when the plane touched down in Atlanta. At home in Buckhead they were greeted with several huge bouquets of flowers. Cooper glanced at the names on the cards but recognized only Matt Dixon's and Gwen's.

It was back to business as usual. Cooper spent long days at the office, sometimes not returning home until after dinner. It didn't matter to Mary Sue who had obligations to one committee or another. She became sought after to the extent that her life apart from Cooper became her only life. She thrived on the admiration of her peers and worked tirelessly to advance her social standing.

When Cooper did arrive home on time, or close to it, Mary Sue had other commitments. He became accustomed to fending for himself, and he started drinking more than he should. He began to delay going home whether he worked late or not, and he became a regular at several spots that were popular with the young professional crowd.

The business lunches and evening cocktails began to take a toll on his midsection. He looked in the mirror one morning and noticed a beer gut straining against the towel wrapped around his waist. That very day he joined the West Paces Racquet Club, a tennis, squash, and workout facility conveniently located just a mile from the house. He disciplined himself and soon established a regimen. Every morning he ran for forty-five minutes on the track that circled the tennis courts. He'd spend another half hour in the weight room, followed by a visit to the sauna. After a shower and a shave he could still be in the office by 9:30.

The West Paces Club also featured a bar and restaurant and it became another of his favorites. In fact, it became a home away from home. He usually occupied his regular stool between six and eight-thirty or nine.

In spite of the exercise regimen, he could not shed his paunch. His features became pasty in appearance, and he fretted over his disintegrating relationship with Mary Sue. One night, after several more drinks than usual, he confided in Dawson Spruill, a bar buddy.

"Man, my marriage is turning to shit. She hardly ever has time to sit and talk, and if she does it's all about her goddamn committees or whatever. If I tell her that I want to take her out somewhere for dinner, she wants to bring her parents along. Christ, I wish we lived a thousand miles away."

Dawson stood two inches taller than Cooper. He wore a thin moustache and had brown eyes and jet-black hair. His suave good looks and conservative dark suits belied his good-humored irreverence.

"Listen old pal, you're from the beach over in South Carolina, right? Why don't you take her there for a long weekend?"

"The only place we could stay is with my family. She doesn't understand them. She thinks they're primitive."

"Don't you own some property down there? It's on an island, isn't it?"

"Well, yeah, Spanish Island. My uncle gave me five acres on the beach for a wedding present."

"Well hell, why don't you build a beach house and surprise her? She may never want to come back to Mommy and Daddy."

Cooper sat silently for several seconds. "Dawson, you know what? That's brilliant. What a great idea! She loves the beach. I love you, but how does a heartless lawyer like you come up with a romantic plan like that?"

"I deal with affairs of the heart every day. Don't forget, I specialize in divorce."

Gwen began to chide Cooper about his appearance and expressed concern that his drinking affected his work. His output for the clients they represented had lost its cutting edge, and displayed a lackluster sameness.

Cooper brushed it off explaining that he was simply in a rut. But at lunch one day he confided that things were not going well between him and Mary Sue. He told Gwen of his plans to surprise her with a house on the beach.

"Coopie, I think that's a great idea. In fact, I think you should take some time off? Go on home for a few days. Get hold of an architect and let it rip. Being away will do you good. I'll look after things here, and when you come back you'll be refreshed."

Three days later, on the pretense that he had to tend to family business, Cooper packed his bag and left for Spanish Island. Mary Sue gave him a peck on the cheek and cautioned him to drive carefully, but she barely noticed he was gone.

After a day with his family, Cooper went to *Ocean Dunes* to visit with Rick and Wendy. Next he went to pay his respects to Carlton Jenkins' but his former employer was out of the country. Then he had a lunch date with Peter Wilson, a friend from College of Charleston, and an architect. Peter had made a name for himself. He designed the really big homes in the area, and several national magazines had showcased his designs.

They reminisced about old times and mutual friends before Cooper explained what he had in mind. He didn't want a simple beach house. He wanted a house that seemed a part of the beach. It would have an unobstructed view of the ocean and be surrounded by a deck. He wanted vaulted ceilings and light, airy rooms. He envisioned curved staircases and a balcony with a railing fronting the guest rooms on the second floor.

"Peter, I want you to bring the outside in."

As they talked, Peter sketched on napkins as his mind sifted subliminally through design concepts that he might employ. After much give and take, they agreed on the basics of a plan for a house that would be unlike any other in the area. In fact, the place would become known as the SS Spanish Island because it would look something like a small, beached ship from several miles at sea.

They met twice more, and when Cooper returned to Atlanta his excitement about the project spilled over. He beamed as he described the basics of the design. He had a healthy tan from his time in the sun, and there was a bounce in his step again.

When Peter's blueprint arrived at his desk two months later Cooper couldn't wait to show it off. He spread it out on the conference room table and proudly pointed out to Matt and Gwen the unique features of the design.

Since his return, his work had regained its focus. He found new purpose to his days, and he eliminated or cut short his visits to his old haunts. Mary Sue's routine remained the same, but Cooper knew her perspective would change once she saw her beautiful place at the beach.

To please her, Cooper came along to the annual Steeplechase, a charity event that combined a social gathering and a horse race set in the rolling hills of a northern suburb. Mary Sue's Junior League chapter had leased a huge motor home for the affair. The thing had restrooms, seating for twenty four, and boasted a full kitchen complete with a refrigerator and icemaker. Two liveried butlers served drinks while two uniformed maids passed plates of hors d'oeuvres.

Once parked at the event, folding tables were set up outside and covered with skirted lace tablecloths. Candelabras flanked silver serving dishes of Lobster Newburg, roast beef, and potatoes julienne. Hearts of palm salad rounded out the buffet that was served on delicate china borrowed from one of the members. Tailgating had never been so elegant, but other groups had similar setups, each trying to outdo the others.

The affair bored Cooper to death. He had nothing in common with the other husbands or escorts who were mostly bankers and lawyers. The horse races were almost an afterthought, but at least they gave him the opportunity to capture some interesting sketches. He drank too much, and on the return trip to Buckhead he fell asleep on one of the couches, lulled by the drone of the engine and the constant chatter. Mary Sue was furious.

Suddenly, the beach house was finished. Peter had outdone himself. Local newspapers featured pictures of the unique structure, and boats full of curiosity seekers were common sights in the water off the beach.

Southern Living asked permission to send a photo crew to capture the architecture and unique decorative treatments for a future issue. Cooper consented with the provision that they provide him with copies of the photos immediately after the shoot. When the glossies arrived a month later, he proudly displayed them around the agency.

"Christ Cooper, you act like you just gave birth," said Gwen.

"I guess in a way I did. Peter and I put our hearts and souls into this project. It started out as a pretty basic idea but it turned out a masterpiece, if I say so myself."

When everyone had seen the pictures Cooper decided to go home for lunch, something he had never before done. He couldn't wait to show the photos to Mary Sue. He imagined her face lighting up, and her impatience to visit the island. They could leave for a long weekend in just a couple of days.

Cooper steered his Porsche into the driveway next to another car, no doubt one of Mary Sue's committee friends. He had hoped to share this moment with her alone. Clutching the folder of photos in one hand and a dozen roses in the other, he entered the house as usual through the garage. Another door led inside to the kitchen where he heard Mary Sue's laughter coming from the back.

Cooper swung open the door to their bedroom and started to shout "surprise" when he saw Mary Sue's clothes strewn around the floor. His eyes darted to the bed where she straddled another man, giggling as she moved up and down. Her face froze as she saw him. She rolled away from her partner and pulled a sheet over her nakedness.

Cooper recognized the man as one of the others from the Steeplechase. He remained motionless for a minute clenching his teeth and staring first at one, and then the other. The man in the bed remained absolutely still, terrified of the look in Cooper's face. Without a word, Cooper approached the bed and threw the roses at Mary Sue. He started to toss the photos as well but changed his mind and walked out of the room.

When Dawson Spruill arrived at the Racquet Club that evening Cooper was already drunk. Cindy, the bar maid, continued to serve him but made sure his refills were mostly water. Dawson dropped into his regular stool.

"Where have you been, old pal? I've missed your ugly mug."

"Dawson, she cheated on me. I found 'em . . . I mean I caught 'em in bed. In *my* bed, goddammit.

"Wait a minute, Coop. Who are you talking about?"

"I'm talking about, Mary Sue, that's who, my wife."

"Mary Sue? Where did you find her?"

"I found her in bed with some guy, tha's where, at my house, in my bed. I should kill the sonofabisch."

"Hold on, old chum. Why don't you come home with me? Let's not kill anyone tonight. It's getting late and you'll have all day tomorrow."

"Dawson, why would she do it? Why? Look at the housh I built for her. She won't ever see it." Cooper pushed the packet of photos towards him.

Dawson flipped through the images. "Wow, this is magnificent. Did you design it?"

"Me and Peter Wilson. He's an archicheck. He's really good."

"I'll say, this place is beautiful."

"Why would she do it, Dawson? Why?"

Two days later Cooper returned home and cleared out his clothing and personal effects. He returned to his old apartment complex in Buckhead and signed a lease on a two-bedroom unit on the ground floor. He spent two hours choosing new furniture at Haverty's, insisting that it be delivered the next day.

He couldn't shake the image of Mary Sue, or the sound of her giggling as she bounced up and down on the man in his bed. He understood, now, that he'd been attracted to her because of what she appeared to be—young, beautiful and socially well-connected. That was just a mirage. In reality, she proved to be callous and conniving. He could never forgive her infidelity. He didn't deserve that. He wanted out. On Dawson's advice he notified the credit card companies where he and Mary Sue had joint accounts. He would no longer be responsible for her charges, and he sued for divorce.

By the weekend he had moved back to his old neighborhood, and began living the single life again. Many of the young women he knew before his marriage were anxious to have a second chance at landing him. Those he hadn't met were eager to make his acquaintance, and he became a regular once more at most of his old haunts.

CHAPTER FOURTEEN

Dixon and Mayfield had reached the top of the heap regionally, but increasingly they were invited to present to major companies in the Northeast. Cooper was in New York one particularly dreary week in February for a preliminary meeting with a prospective client. On Friday he suffered through a boring luncheon at The Palm. His spirits were buoyed by several Stoli martinis served by a waiter in a long white apron and the idea that he would be home in Atlanta by eight o'clock with the whole weekend ahead of him. When the meeting ended he stepped outside to Second Avenue and hailed a cab. Incredibly, one appeared right away. Cooper dubbed it the "the sweet chariot that will carry me home." He began to hum the tune of the old spiritual.

It had started to snow and traffic crept along. He arrived at the airport with just ten minutes to spare only to learn that his flight had not yet left Pittsburgh because of bad weather. The revised estimated departure had moved back to 7 p.m.

"Shit," he muttered, and he left the gate to find the Crown Room. Delta Airlines' VIP Club was just a short walk away. He would find a cozy seat, have a few drinks compliments of the good people at Delta, and await the arrival of his flight.

He found an empty spot at the bar and ordered a Jack Daniels and soda when another unhappy passenger claimed the seat next to him. The man watched the barmaid fix Cooper's drink and said, "I'll have one of the same, pretty lady."

The man looked to be in his forties. He had just a fringe of hair around his temples and looked to be twenty or thirty pounds overweight. He extended his hand. "Hi, Jim Cooney. Who're you."

"Cooper Hamilton." They shook hands. "Where are you headed?"

"Atlanta, then on to Montgomery, but I wouldn't bet any money on it tonight. Everything is all screwed up out there."

"It sure is. Thank God for this place."

"Thank God, and the hundred and fifty bucks it cost to join. But one night like this and it's worth it."

Cooper and Jim Cooney were soon old friends. Without relinquishing their seats at the bar they were happy to order drinks for those standing behind them. When the intrepid gate agent made announcements Jim Cooney would cheer him on. "Let's hear it for Roger Pyle. He tells it like it is, even if it ain't. Pile it on Rog. Let's have a big hand for ol' Rog."

At this point, the agent had to shout over a battery-powered megaphone in order to convey information about even more flight delays and cancellations. It was bedlam. The weather had become worse. All incoming flights were diverted elsewhere, or instructed to stay on the ground where they were. Had New York's finest been confronted with this mob, they would have shrunk to the outer perimeter. Delta employees and the few airport cops in the vicinity of the Crown Room were in over their heads. A brief conference in the corridor involving the District Sales Manager, Roger, and the cops on hand resulted in the decision to close the club at 9 PM. It fell to Roger to break the bad the news.

He walked to the double cherry paneled doors and pulled on one of the polished brass handles. The door opened a crack as the sound of merriment spilled into the otherwise empty gateway outside.

"May I . . . ," Roger's voice cracked over the megaphone. "May I have your attention, please?"

Those closest turned towards him.

"Quiet, please," Roger shouted into the device. "I have an announcement. The Crown Room will close at 9 p.m. That's fifteen minutes from now. The club will close at 9 p.m.."

Silence flowed in waves from the entrance back to the bar as the import of his announcement dawned on the patrons.

"Did he say they're gonna close?" asked one. "Where the hell do we go from here?"

"Yeah," someone else asked, "what do we do, go out and sleep on the curb? Bullshit."

The news worked its way to the bar where Cooper and Jimmy were holding court.

"No way," said Jimmy. "They ain't throwing us out in the cold."

A roar of support drowned out his last words.

"They can't do that to us, can they Cooper?"

Cooper climbed from his bar stool onto the bar and stood unsteadily. He glanced around the room. He held up his hands for quiet. The din diminished as he began to speak.

"Do they think we are livestock? Do they think we will be herded out the door at their bidding. Are we human beings or are we sheep? I ask you again, are we sheep."

A roar erupted, "Hell, no?" and then "Hell no, we won't go. Hell no, we won't go."

"All right, there's our answer," said Jimmy. "The only way we're leaving here is on the seats that we paid for."

The assemblage roared a second time.

"Okay, quiet everybody. Quiet...SHUTUP." Jimmy pointed up to Cooper. "Folks, this is our hero, our savior. We owe him a great debt." Looking up he asked, "what's your name masked man?"

"My name is Buffalo Bob."

A burst of laughter erupted before everyone turned back to their drinks.

At 9:17, the lights blinked out. Security had figured out how to cut the power. With no illumination, no beer flowing out of the tap, and no way to see who you were talking to, the party was over. Roger and his team showed up with flashlights and guided everyone from the darkened premises. It took less than twenty minutes.

The next morning Cooper woke up as boarding passengers shuffled past his spot on the floor. Many seemed to recognize him. They greeted him warmly, "Mornin' Bob," or "Bob, you're our hero." He had the worst hangover of his life, but somehow he made it onto the plane. Halfway through the flight, on his way to the rest room, he spotted Jim Cooney and learned what he had done. He had no recollection of his behavior, and he felt like a fool.

Fortified by three Bloody Marys, Cooper felt somewhat better on arrival in Atlanta. He drove straight home, and after showering and shaving he thought he might live. He pondered how to spend the day when he noticed the red light blinking on the answering machine. He pressed the "play" button and listened.

"Coopie, I've got news." Gwen's voice filled the kitchen. "You should have called in today after your meeting. Call me tonight when you get home if you're still able."

"Shit!" he winced. Gwen had been riding him again about his drinking. Maybe he would call her later in the day. He was suddenly very hungry. He hadn't eaten since yesterday's luncheon meeting. He decided he would go to *Friday's*, and reached for the door when the phone rang.

Gwen asked, "Where the hell have you been?"

He explained about the cancelled flight.

Didn't you get my message?" she asked.

"I just played it. I didn't get home until an hour ago."

"Well, listen to this. Gibbons and Gross wants to buy us out. They'll pay twelve bucks a share."

Her words stunned him. Twelve dollars a share amounted to four times what he had given Donald Mayfield for his stock. He could pay off his loan with the bank and still be worth a few million.

"Jesus, that's great, what did Matt say?"

"He's wants to go for it. He thinks they'll pretty much leave us alone to run things as we want. Basically, they just want a presence in the southeast."

Gibbons and Gross, an international advertising conglomerate based in London, was at the top of the advertising big leagues. They had recently purchased other smaller but highly-regarded agencies in areas they considered underserved. Under their banner, D&M could court even the largest corporate clients. All of a sudden Cooper and Gwen and Matt Dixon were rich.

Six weeks later the papers were signed, the checks distributed, and the three former partners each accepted generous contracts to stay with the agency. On a Monday morning two weeks later, Harris Melville arrived and introduced himself as executive vice president in charge of southeast operations. Cooper disliked him immediately. His clipped British accent dripped with smugness, and his limp handshake and darting eyes lacked sincerity. By noon he had riled most of the other staffers, and announced his plan to take over Dixon's office for himself. Matt saw red.

Over the next few weeks Melville busied himself with administration. He didn't infringe on the creative department. Gwen and Cooper and their colleagues were insulated from him to a degree, but he burdened the account representatives with demands for reports and projections. Morale at Dixon and Mayfield took a nose dive.

CHAPTER FIFTEEN

After more than a year Cooper came home for a long weekend. He stepped off the ferry at the Landing and saw Twilight and a big black stranger at a table on the deck. Cooper started towards them when she saw him and ran to give him a hug.

"Hi Twi. You look great."

"Cooper, we've missed you. You need to come home more often. Say hello to Simon Albury. He's from the Bahamas."

Cooper noticed right away that she spoke in English, not dialect.

Simon stood, sticking out his hand and smiled broadly. "Hi, I'm glad to meet you. I've heard a lot about you."

Cooper liked him right away. He had a genuine smile, and his words were flavored with a gentle lilt. His eyes conveyed honesty and curiosity. He had a clean shave and sported a shirt that overflowed with colorful game fish, something the locals would never wear.

"Sit with us for a while," Twilight patted a spot on the bench next to her.

"Thanks, I will. It's good to be home."

She wanted to hear all about Dixon and Mayfield and asked about Gwen. He brought her up to date before asking about happenings on Spanish Island. He learned that Simon now fished the *Blind Pig* for Uncle Henry. Cooper would like to have talked longer but he wanted to say hello to all the others.

"Well, I'd better go say hey to everyone. Simon maybe we can get together again tomorrow."

"Sorry, I'm heading offshore at dawn, but I'll be back in three or four days."

"I'll be back in Atlanta by then. But maybe we could do some fishing next time I'm down. I haven't wet a line in years."

"I'd like that. Let's plan on it."

Cooper stood, gave Twilight a peck on the cheek and shook hands again with Simon. He walked into Wanda's and surprised her behind her counter. He gave her a hug and chatted for a few minutes before he left to find his uncle. The older man was sitting behind his desk when Cooper opened the door.

"Well, well, look what dropped outa' the sky. I've been wondering if you forgot the way home."

The two embraced before Henry sat back down, and Cooper took a seat facing him. He noticed an adding machine on his uncle's desk.

"When did you start using that thing?"

Henry had never used one before, preferring to keep records of his accounts on legal pads, adding, subtracting and erasing with a pencil. He didn't trust his monthly statements from the bank and would spend as long as it took to reconcile them with long columns of figures on the yellow sheets.

"Well, Wanda uses it. She's been helpin' me with some of the paperwork. Every year we get more damn forms to fill out for the government. It wasn't so bad with just taxes and such, but now we got to report how many tons we caught of this or that. Most of what we get ain't even close to being endangered. It's damn near a full time job just keepin' up with it."

He pulled a fresh White Owl out of his shirt pocket and bit thru the cellophane wrapper. "I got a new man on *Blind Pig*, and we're catching fish we never thought of years ago. We're selling tilefish, monkfish and even dolphinfish, you know, mahi mahi. It's real popular now in some of the fancy restaurants. But how's things with you, son? You're looking well."

Cooper told him about the buyout of the agency. "It was a great deal for Matt and Gwen and me but the guy they sent over from London is a horse's ass."

"Well, what are you fixin' to do? It sounds like you made out pretty good."

"I don't know. It's not the same as it used to be. I used to get all fired up about new accounts and new ideas. Now it's like it all runs together. Sometimes I think I should come home for good. I've got some great ideas for new paintings that I haven't had time to do anything with. I might even buy a boat and do some fishing, maybe even run some charters."

"Well, you know we'd love to have you back."

"Thanks, I might make the break, but not just yet. We've been pitching a major client and I've got to see it through. I can't let Gwen down."

"How is Gwen? She's some little lady? I thought you two worked real good together."

"Gwen's fine. We get along great but the new guy gets under her skin, too." Cooper was curious. "By the way, tell me about Simon. Where did you find him?"

"Well now, that's a story. He come back with me from the Keys on the *Blind Pig*. He's a good man, and him and Twilight are sweet on each other."

"I could see that, but where did he come from?" Cooper persisted.

Henry grunted and released a mouthful of smoke. "I hope you got a few minutes."

He went on to explain that the engine on *Swamp Fox* needed work. He found a yard in Florida that would rebuild it for a reasonable price. The job would take three or four weeks, but he'd have to run the *Fox* to Miami. He decided to bring along *Blind Pig,* as well. He and Karl would spend the time swordfishing in the Gulf Stream off the Keys.

"The Cramer brothers came along. Buddy mated for me and Paul backed up Karl on the *Fox*. They took a bus home from Miami after we got there. Me and Karl caught a bunch of fish that trip. We made enough to pay for the overhaul with some left over to put in the bank."

"Well, the Cramer boys come back down and we headed home. We were in the Stream off Palm Beach when I spotted something white off the starboard bow. I didn't pay it no mind at first but as we got closer, I saw a big dorsal fin circling around it. I figured it must be garbage or something off a ship. When we got closer still it turned out to be one of them big commercial coolers, and then I saw a black arm flop over the top. There was someone hanging on to it, and he had a big ass tiger shark to keep him company."

"It took just a couple of minutes to reach him. Buddy had a rope ladder over the side and a harpoon to fend off the shark. He stuck it once right behind the dorsal, and it took off."

"The guy in the water had just about had it. Me and Buddy had to drag him up the ladder. He collapsed on the deck, but he lifted his head a little and looked straight at me and says, 'Thank you, thank you'."

"Cooper, you know what it's like to be in a fight—a bloody nose here, a black eye there. Well, he wasn't in no fight. He'd had the pure shit beat out of him. One eye was swollen completely shut, his nose bent sideways, and I could tell from the way he held his side when he gagged that he had broken ribs. He was in a world of hurt."

"We cleaned him up as good as we could, and I figured that we'd best get him to a hospital. We could run into Ft. Pierce, drop him off, and put on enough fuel to get us home without another stop. I said as much to Buddy, but he heard me."

"He sat up real slow and said, 'Cap'n, please don't take me to no hospital. Take me where you're going. I won't be no trouble'. What's your name?" I asked him. "He gagged up a little more seawater and told me. I said okay, Simon Albury, what were you doing sailing a cooler around in the middle of the Gulf Stream? He looked at me a little funny and said he must have got lost."

"He didn't beat himself up, and I knew he wasn't out there hanging on to that cooler by his own doin'. I figured we needed to cut him some slack. I had Buddy fix up the bunk in the wheel house where we could keep an eye on him. The two of us carried him in and laid him down and he went out like a light. Next morning about six, I had the helm with my back to him when I heard him stir.

"He said, 'You saved my life,' and he thanked me again."

"We were makin' pretty good time, but we had to put in for fuel. I told him he could leave or he could stay with us on the ride back home."

"He wanted to come along. Said he could see that we had two boats, and if I needed help he could catch me a bunch of fish. Well, something told me he wasn't just blowin' smoke. We fueled up at Mayport and headed back out towards home. Simon sat on the bunk for a while and we talked. He told me how he'd fished all his life, and all about where he grew up in the Abacos. He explained his ideas about the tides and moon stages and such. He knew his shit about fishin'."

Henry took a long drag on the cigar and continued. "So, Simon come home with us. With Karl being so sick, he's been a big help."

"Did you ever find out what happened to him?"

"Coop, he never said a damn word about it."

CHAPTER SIXTEEN

Simon Albury grew up in the northern Bahamas. As a boy he loved to wade and to play in the turquoise water near the beach. He learned to dive and developed the capacity to hold his breath for minutes at a time. He could scoop up three or four conchs from the ocean floor before having to surface for air. Armed with a sling spear, he could surprise a bag full of spiny lobsters or snappers with just a few trips to the bottom.

He practiced the art of casting for bait, and became proficient at throwing a fourteen foot cast net in perfect circles over schools of ballyhoo or goggle eyes. He sold his catch to commercial fishermen and charter captains and soon developed a steady, if modest, income stream. As a side benefit, the Alburys were seldom without fresh seafood for the table.

Simon's natural curiosity made him wonder why fish would strike voraciously at baits one day, and ignore the tastiest offerings the next. He asked others about details of their catches, and compared their experiences with his own. He recorded the data and classified it by time of day, moon phase, tide stage, and water temperature. Over a period of time, patterns emerged that he used to great advantage.

When he was sixteen Robert Culmer, a white captain, asked him to mate for a charter. Culmer's regular mate had gone to Nassau for a few days, and Culmer had booked a convention group on his boat, *Alibi*. Simon jumped at the chance. They would venture offshore in search of marlin, dolphin fish, tuna and wahoo. His experience thus far had been limited to the relatively shallow Sea of Abaco.

He needed little instruction. He knew all about the big rods and reels, and could rig baits as well as anyone. But every captain has an individual technique, and Simon paid close attention as Cap'n Robert explained exactly how he wanted the baits presented to the quarry lurking below.

"The flat lines should drop back to the slope of the second wave. Put the starboard outrigger back on the fourth wave and the port rigger on the fifth. You got it?"

"Yes, sir."

"Okay, and if we hang a big one you put on this glove, and when you grab the leader take only one wrap around it. If I see you take more than one wrap, you are finished with me. Last thing I need is for you to be pulled overboard and dragged under. You hear me?"

"Yes, sir. I surely do."

"One other thing," Culmer regarded him carefully. "If things are slow, we might create a little excitement."

Reaching behind a fish box he produced a banged-up, galvanized garbage can lid thirty inches in diameter. "If I say so, tie a line through the handle of this thing and throw it overboard. It makes more commotion than an army of teasers. I've seen big blues bend these things in half with their bills. And Simon, one more thing, don't ever tell a soul back at the marina about this gadget."

The next morning Simon was on top of the world as he dropped the lines and *Alibi* eased out of her slip. The clients were doctors from South Florida. He produced coffee and doughnuts for the ride offshore and moved about the cockpit like a seasoned veteran. He responded instantly when the captain stomped his foot, a signal for the mate to climb to the bridge for instructions.

Alibi had a different party each of the four days and caught fish every day; mostly wahoo, dolphin, and yellowfin tuna. But the third day proved the most eventful with two blue marlin hooked, and one brought to the boat. Simon followed instructions and brought the fish to gaff without incident. They did not resort to the trash can lid but they would deploy it on many occasions in the future.

After the final trip, Culmer called Simon aside. "How much did you make in tips?" he asked.

Simon suspected the man wanted part of it, but when he responded honestly that he had collected two-hundred forty dollars the captain just whistled and patted him on the back.

"That's great, son. I could tell those doctors liked you. Keeping the clients happy and busy is the secret to this business. You did a fine job."

Two months later Simon became the full-time mate on *Alibi*. He and Culmer soon established a bond not unlike master and apprentice. They had genuine trust and affection for each other, and when Simon's father died, Robert Culmer became his mentor and advisor.

By the time he was thirty, Simon had a reputation as a capable seaman, a first-class mate, and an accomplished mechanic. In between charters he kept busy around the marina. He knew boats inside and out, and it seemed that he could fix even the most vexing mechanical problem. He earned a captain's ticket himself, so he didn't think it unusual when a man he knew only by name asked him to deliver a boat to the States.

Lucas Marley had an unsavory reputation. But Simon knew that he bought and sold boats all the time. Marley operated several boats of the kind used to fish for warm-water lobsters, or "bugs" as they were locally known. He had sold one of the boats, *Abaco Belle*, to a man in Ft. Lauderdale, and delivery was part of the deal. Simon would get $600 plus expenses, and a ticket home on Chalk Airways—pretty good money for a couple of days' work. He accepted the deal.

When Simon did not return from the States as expected, Robert did not worry. There were no charters booked for the week, and he may have decided to spend an extra day or two in Florida before returning. Robert would have bet Simon was hanging around marinas in Ft. Lauderdale learning what he could about the latest fishing tackle and techniques.

Two days later Lucas Marley came around the docks and pointedly asked if Robert had heard from Simon. Marley explained that *Abaco Belle* never arrived in Ft. Lauderdale, and the man he sold her to wanted his money back.

Robert responded that he had not heard from Simon since he left. He went on to make it clear that he would take it very personally if anything should happen to him. Marley backed off, but said, "Let me know if you hear from him".

After a week Robert was deeply troubled. Simon had piloted *Alibi* to Nassau, San Salvador and Miami by himself on many occasions. He knew that Simon would have thoroughly checked the engine and systems on *Abuco Belle* before making the crossing. With nowhere else to turn, he contacted Bahamas Air/Sea Rescue and the U.S. Coast Guard, but neither agency had any record of a distress call involving *Abaco Belle*.

Robert had all but given up hope when six weeks later he received a notice that he had a registered letter. Assuming it to be a deposit on a charter, he waited in line at the post office and put it together with his regular mail to read at home. The envelope bore no return address other than U.S. Post Office, Beaufort, SC.

Later that afternoon as Robert read his mail at the kitchen table, his wife heard him exclaim, "Sweet Jesus, he's alright".

The letter from Simon read:

Dear Captain Robert,

To this day I don't understand just what happened, or why, but the short of it is that I was high-jacked about twenty miles out of West End. They were Hispanics, maybe Cubans or Mexicans. I didn't know it at the time, but there were drugs on board in two duffel bags and that's what they were after.

They were going to kill me when I slipped overboard. I had to swim for it when they blew up the boat and left me for the sharks. I grabbed onto a cooler and somehow hung on. I was beat up pretty badly, but I am much better now. I am staying with the Captain who pulled me out of the water. He gave me work and a place to live. I am quite comfortable for the time being.

My problem is that I don't know who to trust. I don't know if Lucas Marley set this up, or if his buyer in Florida double-crossed him. Maybe somebody else got wind of it and took advantage of the situation. In any case Marley might think that I made off with a lobster boat and a shipment of drugs. If he finds out that I am alive, there will likely be a price on my head. I can't come home until I sort this out, but I had to let you know what's going on with me.

If I might ask a great favor, don't tell anyone else that you have heard from me. Please get word to my mother and sister in Nassau that I am alright. If you need to get in touch with me for any reason, please correspond c/o Captain Henry Parker, Spanish Island, South Carolina.

My very best regards to you and Mrs. Culmer,
Simon Albury

Robert's great shoulders heaved as he exhaled a huge volume of air. He turned to hide the tears welling in his eyes, but his wife had noticed. She came closer to rub the back of his neck.

"I am so thankful" she said softly. "Is he hurt?"

Robert handed her the letter and waited for her response.

"What in the world is going on?" she asked. "We don't have drugs here, do we?"

"No, not in that sense, dear. Bahamians can't afford drugs, but the U.S. market is huge. We are ideally located as a staging point for smuggling the stuff into the States. There's plenty of drug activity offshore. Every day I see boats that have no business being out there and tramp steamers drifting about for no reason."

He continued, "I'll have to get in touch with Mrs. Albury and her daughter. They must be worried to death."

"How will you do that?"

"I'm afraid to use the phone and someone may be watching their mail. I'll just have to pay them a visit. I had planned on going to Nassau in a few weeks but I'll just go sooner.

Part Two

CHAPTER SEVENTEEN

Cooper had been drinking for hours. He decided to quit the agency. The work he once loved had become drudgery. He no longer felt the rush of creativity that sometimes woke him before dawn. Clients were more demanding, and he'd had enough of churning out one inane commercial after another. He would miss Matt and Gwen, but Dixon and Mayfield would have to get along without him. Atlanta had lost its magic, and he had all the money he needed. He would go home to Spanish Island and create significant works of art. On impulse he decided to drive home for a visit and threw some clothes into an overnight bag. He could be at the ferry slip in time to catch the first boat in the morning.

Music on the stereo damped the rhythm of the road as he drove south through the night. His radar detector had not chirped since he crossed I-285, the ribbon of concrete that girds metropolitan Atlanta. Nudging the accelerator, he chuckled as his speed crept up to ninety-five. He loved the performance of the car and the elegance of its design. The Germans sure knew how to build them. He grinned as he raced by other vehicles, weaving from lane to lane. He uncapped a bottle of Jack Daniels and took a long pull, slapping the wheel and singing along with Bob Seger as the dashboard clock advanced to 1:19.

Several miles north of Macon a lighted sign above the pavement alerted traffic to the intersection with I-16, ahead on the left. He eased into the outside lane but did not see a sign warning of construction.

He was changing CDs when his car drifted left on a sweeping curve and burst through a line of orange cones. His hands tightened on the wheel as the tires lost purchase. They bounced on fragments of torn-up pavement and would not turn him back to the highway. He stood on the brake, but it was too late. The car hurtled towards a concrete culvert. He screamed as he exploded through the windshield.

Trooper Michael Dolan surveyed the scene and made a sign of the cross. The car looked like a crushed beer can. Moving his light from side to side, he moved into the waist-high underbrush searching for the victim. Shrubs and nettles tore at his uniformed legs. He slapped at a mosquito and paused when he saw the approaching blue lights of a second cruiser.

The humidity of the early summer morning drenched his shirt. Beads of sweat appeared on his forehead, and ground fog obscured the visibility. He was standing under a tree when his nostrils caught the scent of blood. Something dripped on his head and shoulders, and when he ran his fingers through his hair they came away sticky.

"Oh, shit," he grunted.

He pointed his light overhead. The victim hung from a fork ten feet off the ground.

Paramedics had to use a ladder to reach him, but the man was still alive. They fitted him with a neck collar before lowering him to the ground in a basket. One administered an IV, as two others huddled around him on their knees, struggling to prevent the loss of more blood. In the flashing lights only their backs and the tops of their heads were visible—like players in a furtive game of craps.

Flares lined the highway as radio traffic splintered the silence. Cops in yellow pullovers motioned with flashlights for the light traffic to keep moving; but the cars crept by, their occupants peering into the gloom, compelled to look but afraid of what they might see.

He stank of booze. His legs were broken and twisted, and he had lost a critical volume of blood. The gash on his forehead suggested a concussion, and obviously he had internal injuries. If they didn't get him to the hospital fast he wouldn't have a chance. It was a good bet they'd lose him anyway.

"Let's load him up," ordered one. The three figures re-grouped around him. "Okay, all together now, lift!"

They jockeyed the gurney into the back of the ambulance where it locked in place. The cops halted traffic and escorted the vehicle back onto the highway. As it sped away, the driver switched on the siren almost as an afterthought.

A second trooper took photos while Dolan filled out the incident report. He had retrieved a license from the driver's wallet, and the registration from the glove box. The car was a silver 1982 Porsche registered in Fulton County to the victim, Cooper Hamilton of 2317 Vienna Circle, N.E., Apt.121, Atlanta.

Dolan radioed a request that an officer be dispatched to notify family members.

He continued with the report, filling in the blanks: White, Male, Thirty-seven, Clear and Dry, Speeding and likely DUI, Extensive and maybe fatal. He had just finished when the wrecker arrived. The driver stepped down from the cab.

"Damn, this looks like balled up tin foil."

"It's a mess, that's for sure."

"Was they all killed?"

"There was just one. He's alive but not by much."

Dolan had a last look inside and collected the three biggest pieces of the bottle. He put them in an evidence bag and signaled all clear.

The operator attached a cable to the underside before winching the wreck onto the cantilevered truck bed. After he secured it with chains Dolan escorted him back onto the highway, and minutes later the flashing lights of the two cruisers blinked off as they departed the scene also.

At 2:03 a.m. the EMTs wheeled their patient into the pale green interior of the emergency room. The nurse in charge signed off on the patient care report and paged the solitary emergency room doctor. She was checking her new patient's blood pressure when the cardiac monitor next to the gurney emitted a shriek. Cooper's heart stopped beating at 2:08.

"I need some help over here now," she bellowed.

She began CPR. After a full minute she paused, but no activity registered on the monitor. Another nurse appeared with a defibrillator on a cart. The two of them cut away what remained of his shirt and held the paddles to his chest.

"Okay, stand back," ordered the first. As she pushed a button, Cooper's body twitched on the gurney, but the flat line on the monitor continued its path across the screen.

"Again," she announced. His face was pasty pale as the voltage surged through him a second time. The display on the monitor remained unchanged.

"We'll try one more time." She checked to make sure the electrodes made good contact with his skin. "Okay, here goes."

His form jumped again with no result.

"Oh dear, we've lost him."

Twilight sat upright in bed. Her black eyes blinked, and her breathing became labored. Outside her screened window palmettos stood like sentries in the light of a half-moon in the cloudless sky. The only sound came from a chuck-wills-widow. She had been summoned by the Spirits. As if being spun into a vortex, she began to comprehend that someone she loved hovered near death.

Simon was fishing offshore, but he had good weather. He would be alright. With a hand to her throat she gasped, "It must be Cooper."

She hurried through the house to the shallow box on the lace-covered table in the front room. She touched a match to the wicks of the two tall candles beside it before removing its contents: three vials of powder and a jar containing twelve wooden beads the size of marbles. Six were white, and six were black. She cast the black orbs into the box and watched as they rolled to rest. After sprinkling the beads with white powder she opened a drawer and withdrew a white wax taper. She held it up to one of the candles and watched as its flame came to life. Holding it with both hands, she sat in silence until it burned itself out.

Cooper felt like a boy again, bobbing in his skiff on a peaceful sea. Gentle swells undulated beneath him. He could hear no sound, but the sun hurt his eyes. He tried to turn away, but his arms and legs would not respond. He squinted, but the brilliance began to fade. It moved away slowly at first, then accelerated and streaked across the sky until it appeared as a mere speck on the horizon. Segments of his life began to flicker in his consciousness. The images were realistic, not crazy or exaggerated like nightmares.

He found himself in a place that seemed colder and quieter than he thought possible. He wondered if he might be dead, but it did not matter. He felt utterly at peace. Then he came to the entrance to a tunnel. At the far end he could see a radiance that changed hues like a kaleidoscope. Hauntingly beautiful music tempted him to enter, but the vaguely familiar image of a man appeared at the center of the passage. He did not speak, but somehow Cooper understood his thoughts, "Go back, it is not your time." The man gestured for him to turn around. "Go back," he communicated again, before disappearing.

The tunnel vanished. Cooper was drifting again in his skiff. He had no idea how long he had been there, but at some point the light reappeared. Bright sunshine bathed his boat. He felt its warmth on his face and his shoulders. It cheered him. The cold evaporated and he sensed movement. He heard ripples lapping at the hull, and he could smell the sea.

The nurse mouthed a silent prayer as she unfolded a sheet and draped it over her patient. She had started back to her station when the monitor emitted a single beep. She spun around. Another beep followed, and then the machine began to signal the slow but regular spasms of her patient's heart.

"We have a pulse," she exulted as she regarded Cooper's battered face. "Okay mister, we got you back. The rest is up to you. Just stay with us."

CHAPTER EIGHTEEN

Cooper's eyes blinked open. He moaned and attempted to turn on his side, but a nurse noticed his movements.

"Stop! You've got to lie still."

"What happened?" he rasped.

"You're in a hospital. You had a terrible accident."

Rose Harris was a native of middle Georgia. She had little sympathy for drunks, but her professional instincts overrode her personal feelings. She moved to his side to give him a few sips of water from a straw. She waited while he swallowed.

His words were barely a whisper, "How long have I been here?"

"Since Monday, you're badly hurt."

"What day is today?"

"It's Friday," she said removing the straw from his lips.

"Where am I?"

"At the Medical Center of Central Georgia."

"Where is that?"

"In Macon, Macon Georgia."

"Does anyone know I'm here?"

"Well, three days ago a tall, red-haired lady came in with an older man and a black woman. They spent quite some time talking with Dr. Bennett. They brought you those flowers over there."

"Did my mother come with them?"

Miss Harris checked his blood pressure. "Your mother wasn't here."

"She spoke to me. You must have seen her. She has white hair."

"You were under sedation, you know, unconscious. You couldn't have seen anyone. I saw only the three I mentioned. I'm sure I'd remember an older woman with white hair, but I didn't see anyone like that. Excuse me, but Dr. Bennett told me to call right away if you . . . with any change in your condition. I'll be right back. Try not to move. You have internal injuries."

She walked to the end of the ward and picked up a phone. Within minutes the tall, gaunt doctor appeared at his bed with

Miss Harris trailing behind. His bony arms were too long for the sleeves of his white jacket and his glasses rested on the tip of his nose.

"Well Hamilton, if you were trying to end it all, you screwed up. Anyone else who drank a quart of Jack and drove into an immovable object would be just so much road kill, but not you. No sir, you go flying through the air and land in a tree like a goddamn kite. Then they bring you in here and we have to put you back together like Humpty Dumpty. It's hard for me to believe you're here looking at me. How you made it through those first few days is beyond my comprehension.

Miss Harris shrank from Cooper's bedside and busied herself with another patient.

"By the way, I'm Jake Bennett. I'm a surgeon. I had to figure out where you were bleeding internally. Forgive my language, Hamilton, but I spent two years in Vietnam patchin' guys up who wanted nothing more than to go home. A lot of them didn't make it. I just need to know if you want to live or if I wasted my damn time."

He did not wait for an answer. "Your partner Gwen is some lady. She and your uncle and Twilight all care a lot about you. You owe it to them to straighten yourself out."

"When did my mother come?" Cooper interrupted.

"I only saw the other three."

"But my mother had to be here. I know it. She talked to me."

"Well, medication does strange things to the mind. We'll talk again tomorrow, Hamilton. Right now you need to sleep."

They moved Cooper to another floor the following afternoon. An orderly wheeled his gurney to the elevator along with a stand holding the IV's dripping into his arm. Miss Harris followed with his chart, his personal effects, and the flowers from his family. She left them at the nurses' station on seven and hurried back to the elevator. It was time for her break.

The duty nurse waved a thank you and started to log in her new patient when she glanced at the flowers on the counter. An object hid amidst the stems of the blooms. She reached up and plucked it out. It was a doll, just six inches tall, the image of a pretty, smiling woman with blue eyes and white hair. It had life-like facial characteristics, and wore a tiny dress.

She was intrigued and turned it in her hands as the emergency call sounded. The red light above Room 714 flashed on her console. She put the doll on the counter and started down the hall, knowing already that Mrs. Poteat had passed away.

The ward supervisor arrived a few minutes before eight to take charge until morning. She exchanged greetings with other staffers and glanced at the charts in the rack. There were fourteen. She looked over the activity log noting the discharge of three patients and the admission of one. All was quiet on the floor. The doctors had gone and there were no visitors. She applied lotion to her hands as her eyes strayed to the end of the counter and fixed on the doll. Curious, she moved closer.

She stared open-mouthed at the likeness and recognized it right away. Her eyes darted back to the chart rack. "Oh, my God, there it is, HAMILTON, oh Lord."

She hurried down the hall to 703 where a figure lay still in the darkened room. Bandages obscured the forehead, and sheets covered the torso to the neck line. She walked to the bedside and whispered, "Poor Ettie, what in the world happened to you?"

"Who are you?" a male voice croaked.

"Oh, I'm sorry. I've made a mistake. I thought you were Ettie Hamilton."

"I'm Cooper Hamilton."

Her knees weakened. She grabbed hold of the bed to steady herself. "Cooper, oh my God. Cooper it's me. It's me Kathleen. I saw the name, and I thought it was your mother, not you."

He lay quiet as he struggled to focus on her face. "Kathleen? Kathleen Grimes? Why . . . what are you doing here?

"I work here. I've been here for ten years."

Peering from underneath the bandages his eyes, slow from the morphine, found hers. The pert ponytail he remembered was gone. She now wore a pageboy, and small gold rings hung from her ears. Instead of shorts and a T-shirt, she wore blue scrub pants and a bright print top. Lines had begun to form at the corners, but her eyes were the same amazing blue.

"Kat, you haven't changed. You look great."

She stifled a gasp and folded her arms to steady herself.

"You've got to sleep. I'll be back a little later," she managed before hurrying out the door.

Her tears came in torrents. She fled to the break room and paced until her sobbing subsided. Her emotions were overwhelmed with the still-painful memory of her bitter divorce, and now the shock of finding Cooper on her floor. The sound of his voice cried out to something deep in her being that had withered years ago. The intensity of her feelings unsettled her. Just as her life was leveling out, here was another upheaval. She froze as a sudden thought raced through her mind. Could he possibly know about the child?

CHAPTER NINETEEN

Kathleen regained her composure. She dried her eyes, combed her hair and returned to her station. She reached immediately for Cooper's chart to learn the extent of his injuries.

"Oh Lord, cardiac arrest." Her hand covered her mouth as she read every notation and scribbled comment before replacing the folder in the rack. She felt the tears coming again but bit her lip as her colleague returned.

"Oh, Hi Kathleen. I didn't see you come in. Mrs. Poteat passed. I've been in her room."

"I just came from 703."

"Oh yeah, that one's pretty banged up. By the way, when they brought his things down I found a little doll stuffed in his flowers. Well, where did it go? I left it right there on the desk."

"I have it, Marcy. It's a likeness of Ettie Hamilton, our patient's mother. I knew her a long time ago."

"Gee, what a small world, but wow, what a funny place to keep a doll, especially a doll of your own mother. What do you make of that?"

"I'm not sure."

Kathleen returned to Cooper's room just after 10 p.m. "Hi, how are you feeling?"

"I'm ready for my shot," he rasped.

I talked to Dr. Bennett. He seemed surprised that I know you. He said he was a little rough on you at first and he's sorry. He said that your Uncle Henry came here with Twilight and another woman."

"I know. She's my partner, Gwen, but my mother came, too. She took my hand and talked to me. I heard her voice for the first time in my life. She wouldn't let me go to sleep. She sat there by my side all night. Every time I'd start to drift off she'd squeeze my hand and keep me awake. The next thing I knew it was daylight, and she had gone."

Kathleen showed him the doll. "Cooper, she didn't come. We found this in the flowers they brought down with your things."

"I heard her speak, I remember her words. I know what her voice sounds like. That could not have been a dream."

"I know you believe that, but she was not here."

As he stared at the doll, she watched the disappointment mount as comprehension dawned behind his eyes.

He looked at her, "I had this crazy dream. I was floating in the air looking down on myself in a boat, and then I was in front of a tunnel that opened into lights and music. I was drawn to it, but a man appeared and made me turn around. He didn't say anything, but somehow I could understand his thoughts. He looked familiar. I couldn't place him at the time, but I think it was my father. He looked like the picture my mother keeps in her room."

He said nothing for a minute before he continued, "It's all because of Twilight, isn't it? My mother didn't come."

Kathleen struggled to hold back her tears. "No, she didn't, but Twilight made her appear to you. She saved your life. It's a miracle you survived the first few days.

Kathleen administered his medication and tucked the call button into his hand. "Try to rest. I'll be right down the hall if you need anything."

"Kathleen, do you remember us?"

She could take no more. Tears streamed down her cheeks as she nodded and ran from the room.

Jake Bennett appeared at Cooper's side the next day. "How're you feeling Hamilton? Your vitals look good and the legs seem to be coming along okay. We're going to get you into therapy pretty soon."

"What does that mean?"

"You're going to have to start to walk. Otherwise your muscles will atrophy. We have to build them back up."

"I might be wrong, Hamilton, but given the amount of booze in your system when they brought you in you must be a binge drinker. Over time the body builds up a resistance to it. That's the only way you made it as far as Macon. Do you get drunk every day?"

"No, I . . . "

"I'll tell you something else. I'm a recovering alcoholic. When I got back from 'Nam I drank myself into a stupor every night just so I could sleep. I wouldn't eat, I didn't want to socialize, and I was killing myself. But medicine's the most important thing in my life, and I realized if I didn't quit drinking I could kiss it goodbye. So I went to see a priest. Turns out he was in the same boat. He introduced me to his group, all of them recovering just like I am. It's the only thing that saved my life, and my career."

"What does that have to do with me?"

"Hamilton, you might not realize it but you're a drunk. I know the pattern. You blame the pressure at work, your divorce, everything but yourself. Some of us just don't know when enough is enough. We're not like normal people who can have a drink or two and let it go at that. We gotta keep going until we finish the whole fucking bottle. It's a disease. There's no remedy but to quit drinking, and even then we're not cured, we're just okay until we break down and take another drink. This is a damn fine hospital, and we can make you whole again but what's the point if you're gonna kill yourself."

"That's all I'll say. I won't push you. In fact, as a group we don't try to help until someone asks for help, but if I were you Hamilton I'd take a hard look at myself. What about your family? Think about them."

CHAPTER TWENTY

Cooper's therapy started on a Monday when an unfamiliar face appeared at his bedside.

"Hi, I'm Ellen Walker, your physical therapist, and no cracks about my name. I've heard 'em all."

Cooper managed a smile. She was pleasant looking, in her late thirties, solid but not fat. She sat on the edge of his bed and cleaned her glasses.

"Okay, let's start with a few questions. You've been here now for almost two weeks, is that right?"

"I guess. It's easy to lose track."

"How much do you weigh?"

"One eighty."

"And you're what, about six feet?"

"Five-eleven."

"Okay, what we've got to do is get you on your feet. It doesn't look like there's any nerve damage, so we're lucky there. Your bones are knitting back together, and they're still fragile. But we can't allow your muscles to get any weaker. It's a painful process and you may want to kill me, but if you hang in there, I'll get you through it."

"We'll start by getting you to sit up on the edge of the bed. I'll put the walker in front of you and help you to stand. We'll do that several times until I'm sure you won't fall. That'll do it for today. Tomorrow we'll take a short step or two and a few more the next day. By Friday, I want you to be able to get to the bathroom and back by yourself."

Cooper sat up, supporting himself on his elbows, "When will I be able to walk on my own again?"

"Let me finish. Next we'll fit you for crutches, and we'll take little walks down the hall. Then you'll start on water therapy. We've got a great whirlpool. The water is warm, and it helps to support you so there won't be as much weight on your legs. That's how it goes for starters. Now, any questions?"

"How long until I won't need crutches?"

"That depends on your determination, you know, how much effort you give it. And some people just naturally heal quicker than others. I can't give you a timetable."

"How much longer will I be here?"

"I'd say three weeks to a month. Let's face it, your legs weren't just broken, they were mangled. You're lucky you didn't lose them. We've got a lot of work to do. Well, they're coming around with lunch now, so I'll come back at two thirty and we'll take it from there."

At that moment Gwen appeared at the door. She had fixed her red hair up in a French twist accented by large gold earrings, and she wore a tailored black suit with an ecru silk blouse open to her cleavage.

"Am I interrupting something?"

"Oh, no. We're finished. Hi, I'm Ellen Walker. I'm your husband's physical therapist."

Gwen was secretly pleased that she appeared young enough to be married to Cooper. "I'm Gwen Easterly. I'm just his partner not his wife, thank God. I brought a few things from the office so his mind won't turn to mush."

"We'll, I'll be back after lunch. It's nice to meet you."

"You too, bye Ellen."

Gwen looked at Cooper, "You sure look better than the last time I saw you."

"Thanks, you look great, too."

"Cooper, I'm serious. We were so worried. The doctor didn't give us much hope. I felt so awful for your uncle and Twilight."

"I guess I was pretty lucky. What did you bring from the office?"

"Just a storyboard for the *Grapevine Bay* shoot, the copy needs something but I can't put my finger on it. I thought you might give it a new slant." She reached in her portfolio and produced it. "Look at this. It sucks. We need to punch it up somehow."

She held it up for Cooper to see as Kathleen entered the room. She wore a simple, pale yellow pant suit with a white blouse and pearls. Matching earrings and white sling back shoes completed her outfit.

"Oh, sorry, I didn't realize that you had company."

"It's okay Kat, this is my partner." Cooper introduced them, explaining to Gwen that Kathleen normally works the night shift.

"By the way, why are you here at this time of day?" he asked.

"We have a department meeting every month and today's the day. It just broke up and I thought I'd look in on you."

A volunteer wheeled a meal cart into the room as Kathleen started to leave.

"I see it's lunchtime, so I'll leave you two to visit."

"No, wait Kathleen," said Gwen. "I have to go, too. I'll walk out with you. Bye bye, Coopie. Behave yourself. I'll call you tomorrow about Grapevine Bay."

The two women left the room together.

"Christ, I'm starving," Gwen said. "Will you join me for a quick bite somewhere?"

"Well, I've got some errands to run, but sure, there's a place just up the block. It's called *Transfusions*."

They took the elevator to the ground floor and exited to the street. Both drew admiring glances from the men in the lunchtime crowd as they made their way to the café. They chose a table in a quiet corner.

"Let's have a glass of Chardonnay," Gwen suggested.

"It's a little early for me."

"Oh, come on Kathleen. Let's let our hair down and talk about our boy."

Gwen ordered the wine.

"What do you mean by our boy?"

"Kathleen, cut the bullshit. Cooper told me about you. I saw the way you two looked at each other. It's obvious that he's crazy about you and that it's mutual. I love him too, but in a different way. Let's face it, I'm eight years older than he is. I'm sorry. I didn't mean to come on so strong. I guess I've been living in a man's world too long."

The waiter returned to take their order. They both chose the special—a cup of vichyssoise and smoked salmon with capers on a bed of romaine lettuce.

"We'd like some more wine please," Gwen added. Kathleen started to protest but realized it would do no good.

They enjoyed an easy exchange over the next two hours. Gwen described her routine working with the agency and explained the process of creating advertising campaigns.

"Cooper is great to work with. We came up with some pretty neat stuff together, but I think the glamorous world of advertising has lost its magic for him. Clients just squeeze and squeeze until there's nothing left, but he's got talent most people can only dream of. You should see the work he did in Europe. He's lost confidence in himself, but I know he can get it back."

Gwen admitted that she, too, had become disillusioned with the agency. "It was different when it was just the three of us, but the Brits can only see the bottom line. Now it's like working in a goddamn hardware store. However, I've had a few offers, so I might be making a change before too long."

As they became more comfortable with each other, Kathleen lost her usual reticence. She recounted the story of her marriage to a philandering doctor. After he promised repeatedly never to stray again, the late night phone calls from his girlfriends continued. She realized he would never change and filed for divorce. It was ugly. His attorney produced sordid photos of a look-alike in an effort to discredit her. She got her divorce, but he kept the house, and the Mercedes, and his considerable portfolio. She didn't care, she just wanted to be rid of him.

"Did you know Cooper's wife?" she asked Gwen suddenly.

"Mary Sue? Ooh yeah, a self-consumed little bitch."

Gwen related what she knew about the relationship and the circumstances leading to the the breakup.

"That marriage was doomed from the start. But enough said about that, tell me about Cooper's prognosis? What happens now?"

"Well, he's got to get through therapy. It's painful, but it's the only way he'll regain the use of his legs."

"Will he ever walk normally again?"

"Doctor Bennett thinks the chances are good."

Gwen glanced at her watch. "Oh shit, it's 2:45. I've got to get back to Atlanta. Kathleen, I'm so glad I had a chance to get to know you. I hope we can stay in touch. I know you and Cooper will be great for each other and I wish you both the very best."

"Aren't you rushing things a little? We hadn't seen each other in thirteen years."

Gwen just winked. They stood together and Kathleen extended her hand, but on impulse the two embraced.

"Keep me posted, okay?" Gwen offered her card to Kathleen.

"Of course."

"Promise?"

"I Promise."

CHAPTER TWENTY-ONE

At 2:35 Ellen came back. An aluminum walker preceded her through the door. "Well, I see you haven't tried to escape. Are you ready to start?"

"I guess I don't have much choice," said Cooper.

Ellen positioned the walker next to the bed. "I want you to sit on the side and grasp the handles. Then slowly transfer your weight from the bed to the walker. See if you can touch the floor with your feet."

He shifted his position so that his feet just brushed the cool tiles.

"Good, very good. Okay, now gradually put more weight on your legs."

Beads of perspiration formed on his forehead as Cooper did as she asked. He grimaced as his legs bore more of the burden.

"That's it. That's good! Now, transfer your weight back to the bed and we'll call it a day."

"I want to take a step first."

"We need to take this slowly. We can't rush it."

"Just one step, then I'll get back in bed."

"Well, go easy and hold tight to the walker."

Cooper steeled himself before moving his right leg forward. He shifted his weight and brought the left leg forward as well. Ellen watched the determination in his eyes. This one would make her job easy, she thought. In fact, she might have to hold him back.

By the third day Cooper could make his way to and from the toilet. That evening when Kathleen came in he stood at the window with the aid of the walker.

"You're up, how great," she beamed. "You deserve a prize."

"How about a kiss?" he responded.

Kathleen's smile vanished. She stood silently for a minute before crossing the floor. She put her arms around his neck and kissed him softly.

His voice was husky. "Kat, do you think we could start again where we left off?"

"I don't know. It's been so long."

"Don't you want to give it a try?"

"Give me a little more time. This has all been very sudden."

"I've always wondered why you quit writing. Did you meet some other guy?"

She moved to the bed and straightened the covers. "No. My parents made me stop."

He looked at her with a quizzical expression. The images of her straight-laced mother and her bearded father flashed in his mind. He let it go at that.

They released Cooper from the hospital three weeks later. Henry and Melanie drove to Macon to pick him up, and Kathleen came in to see him off. Henry pecked her cheek, and Melanie embraced her. "Child you haven't aged a day. I just can't believe it's been so long."

"Oh, thank you. I've thought about you all so often. You both look wonderful."

Ellen Walker appeared with a wheel chair but Cooper held up his hand. "I'm walking out of here on my own."

"You didn't walk in, and you can't walk out. Sorry but it's hospital policy."

Kathleen interceded, "She's right, Cooper, it has to do with liability. Be nice and do as she says. Ellen I'll wheel him down. I'm sure you're busy."

"Thanks Kathleen, I'm overdue in water therapy." She turned to Cooper and held out her hand. "I wish all my patients were like you. Best of luck, and come see us if you have a chance."

"Ellen, thanks for everything. I promise I'll be back for a visit." Cooper backed into the chair and Kathleen pushed him out of the room past the desk where the nurses all waved and wished him well. When the elevator doors opened downstairs in the lobby, Henry went to get the car.

"Kathleen, won't you come for a visit?" asked Melanie. "Everyone would love to see you, especially Wanda, and Twilight. They both send their love."

Kathleen looked at Cooper. "I will. I'd love to see everybody, and I do have some leftover vacation."

"Oh, good. I'll tell them."

Kathleen wheeled Cooper out the front door to the car at the curb. He stood, using his crutches for support and held out his arms. Kathleen came to him and they embraced. He held her tightly and whispered, "I'll call you tonight, okay?"

"Okay," she murmured before she kissed him lightly on his lips.

The ride took longer than it should have. Cooper's legs cramped up, and Henry had to pull over several times to let him stretch. He had mastered the crutches and could get in and out of the car on his own, but Melanie fretted over him.

Once aboard the ferry he insisted on standing outside over her objections. He balanced on his crutches next to the rail and savored the salt air. He would be home in just minutes. Except for his legs, he was in pretty good shape. He'd lost a few pounds and his pallor had vanished. He looked healthy again, and he hadn't had a drink since the night of the accident.

Several times he had thought about Jake Bennett's words, "you're a drunk . . . not like normal people . . . gotta finish the whole fucking bottle."

He thought about the times he'd spent all night drinking, only to wake the next morning with no recollection of where he'd been. He winced as he recalled Jim Cooney's account of his behavior in the Crown Room at LaGuardia and wondered if he really had a problem. One day at the hospital he had asked to speak with Dr. Bennett. Hours later the tall doctor strode into his room.

"Hello, Hamilton. How's the therapy coming along?"

Cooper reached for his crutches and got to his feet. "Pretty good, I guess. Ellen seems pleased with my progress."

"That's fine, that's what I hear. I understand you wanted to see me. What about?"

"I've been thinking about what you said, you know, about me being a drunk. I guess you might be right about that, but it's been over a month since I had a drink and I don't miss it. If I don't have a physical addiction why would it be so hard for me to quit drinking on my own?"

"You've been in a controlled situation. You don't miss it because you can't get it here and you know it. But what happens after you leave and have a bad day at work, or something's got you down? That's the problem. That's when you'll need a support group or you'll head straight for the nearest gin mill."

"I guess I'm pretty lucky. I've been given a second chance at life, and I hope I'm going to get a second chance with the only woman I've ever really loved. She's my support group. That's all I need."

"Well, I've read the reports from Miss Walker about your therapy. She thinks you're one determined son of a bitch, and I can see it in your face. Some people can handle recovery on their own. Maybe you're one of them. I hope so, but if you fall on your ass I'm as close as the phone, and by the way, call me Jake."

The sound of the intercom in the hall interrupted the conversation. "Dr. Bennett, please report to surgery. Doctor Bennett to surgery."

"Ah shit, got to go." Jake Bennett produced a business card and jotted down his home number.

"If you can't reach me here at the hospital, call this number. Leave a message if I'm not there. Good luck to you Hamilton. I'll be pulling for you."

"Thanks for everything Jake, and call me Cooper." They shook hands.

As the ferry turned into the channel, pluff mud on the creek bank released its unmistakable odor. It signaled to Cooper that he was truly home, in the place where his soul was centered. Karl waved from his wheel chair above on the deck, as Twilight, Simon and Wanda waited impatiently on the dock. When the ferry tied up they hurried forward to help him disembark. Once on the dock he maneuvered with the help of his crutches, but they weren't much help on the ramp. Instead, he supported himself with the railing and made it to the deck on his own. Cooper shook hands with Karl as they all gathered around one of the tables. Wanda disappeared for a few minutes, and returned with a pitcher of icy, sweet tea and paper cups. The tea refreshed, but it did little to temper the humidity and low-nineties heat of the early afternoon.

Melanie realized that Cooper must be worn out. "I'm sure you're anxious to get home. Twilight and I went over and checked the place yesterday. Everything is fine."

"I am a little tired. I guess I could use a nap."

Twilight stood up. "Simon and I will run you over. He can help you up the steps. They're a lot steeper than the ramp."

"We'll be over a little later with some supper," Melanie piped up. "We'll bring your mother along. You go ahead and get some rest."

Twilight helped Cooper into the front seat of the cart where he would have more room for his legs. Simon had to stop by the office so they had a few minutes alone. She sat quietly, but after a minute she looked at him.

"Do you know how close you came to killing yourself?" Before he could answer she went on. "The doctor told us you were drunk when you had the accident. Is that so?"

"I won't lie to you, Twi. I was smashed. I made up my mind to leave the agency and I started drinking. I decided to come home for a visit but I should have waited until the next day."

"Do you have a problem with drinking?" she persisted.

"Yes. I mean no. I haven't had a drop since that night and I don't miss it, but I'm giving it up."

"Do you mean that?"

"I'm going to ask Kathleen to marry me. When I do, I'm going to promise her that I will never take another drink. I mean it."

Her dark eyes softened and wrinkled at the corners as her face broadened into a smile. "Oh Coop, that's so nice to hear. I always thought you two were perfect for each other. I'm very happy." She caressed his cheek.

Simon drove the cart to the house and pulled up next to the stairs. He helped Cooper to his feet, supporting him until he had hold of the railing. Cooper took a tentative first step, "let me try this on my own." He made it to the third step before one leg buckled and he tumbled backwards landing on the sand. His face contorted in pain.

"Oh Baby, are you okay?" Twilight was on her knees next to him. "Simon you'll have to help."

Simon kneeled with his back to Cooper, "Put your arms around my neck. I'll give you a piggy back ride." The big man slowly got to his feet, lifting him off the ground. He put his forearms under Cooper's knees and turned before climbing the steps. Twilight followed with the crutches and opened the unlocked door. Cooper made his way to one of the big couches and sat down.

"Thanks, Simon. I forgot about those stairs. I guess I'll have to stay up here for a while."

Simon walked back to the door. "I've got an idea." He looked out at the design of the staircase. "I think I can rig up a lift. With counterweights it could run on an electric motor and you could operate it yourself. When you don't need it any longer, we can just take it down. Have you got some paper and a pencil?"

Twilight produced scratch pad from a drawer and Simon made a rough sketch of what he had in mind.

Cooper became animated as he grasped the concept. "Sure, that would work. All we have to do is knock out the railing on one side." He took the pencil and added a few lines as he spoke. "We could build an A-frame like this that would support the pulleys. We just need some lumber."

"There's some old wood in the storeroom we could use. I've got a couple of days before my next trip, so I could start tomorrow. It won't take more than ten or twelve hours."

Cooper stifled a yawn. "That's great, and I can help."

Twilight stood up. "You need to get some rest. Let's get you into your room. Simon, I'll be here for a day or two. You take the cart."

After Simon left she guided Cooper into his room and turned down the covers. She helped him into the big bed and pulled a sheet over him. "You just rest. I'll be on the deck if you need anything."

"Thanks very much, and Twi, the doll that they found in the flowers . . . Kathleen told me about it. It saved my life. She's keeping it for me."

She leaned down and kissed his forehead before leaving the room.

Twilight sank into one of the big rockers on the deck that faced the ocean. The afternoon sea breeze cooled her as she watched the sparkling waves. She sat quietly for several minutes before beginning to pray. "Lord, thank you for sparin' he. He ain't deserve to die so young. He ain't stray no mo.'"

After a time she took a letter from her pocket. The envelope was creased and dog-eared. She read it again although she knew the words by heart.

Dear Miss Pinckney,

I have been retained to investigate the possibility of purchasing property in your area. Because your land fronts the Spanish River, it is attractive to my client. Our research indicates that although you do not have clear title, you are an heir to the estate of your great-grandfather, Hosea Pinckney. As such, you can sell your partial interest in the property whenever you like.

A petition to the Court will involve many hours of research, and the preparation of numerous legal briefs. Attorneys' fees could amount to many thousands of dollars. With that in mind, my client has instructed me to offer you the sum of $50,000 for your property with the understanding that he will absorb the cost of all legal proceedings necessary to effect the sale. That will leave you with the entire amount to spend as you wish.

My client is anxious to move quickly on this matter and is considering other properties, as well. If you are interested in his very generous offer, I urge you to act quickly.

Please contact me directly at my Beaufort office.

The letter was signed by David G. Trask, Esq. and had arrived a week earlier. Twilight returned the letter to its envelope. She could not understand the suggestion that she did not have title to her property. She would ask Cooper about it, but she would wait until he felt better.

They heard a clatter at the back of the house the next morning as Simon unloaded the lumber from the storeroom. Cooper stood on his crutches at the door and insisted on watching as Simon fashioned two long uprights. One at a time, he tied a rope around the ends and pulled them up from the top of the steps. Once in position he cross-braced them to form vertical supports that along with the existing stairwell would form a shaft. It would accommodate a small elevator with a floor, but no walls or roof. The weight of the platform and its passenger would be counterbalanced by a stack of cinderblocks. To descend, Cooper would step in and hold the switch in the down position. The car would slowly descend to the ground where he could step off. To ascend he would simply hold the switch up.

Cooper watched every step and helped to the extent that he could. He and Simon began an easy friendship. When they weren't concentrating on the work at hand, they swapped stories about fishing. Cooper was absorbed with Simon's experiences on *Alibi*, and he announced his plan to buy a sport fishing boat when his legs were strong enough. They debated the relative merits of several makes of boats and the equipment they considered necessary. Neither tired of the subject. They both loved blue water, and the prospect of prowling the Gulf Stream together quickened their pulses.

Simon finished the project by noon of the second day. He made the electrical connections, and now they had to test the contraption. He mounted the stairs and watched as Cooper stepped into the lift. Twilight looked out the open door as Cooper held the switch down and slowly descended out of view.

"This is great," they heard him shout.

Simon bounded down the stairs to check the alignment of the car with the shaft, but it needed no adjustment. It jolted a bit when it reached the ground, but that was to be expected.

Cooper laughed. "Great job Simon, this thing is a work of art." He stepped back in and rode the top of the stairs.

CHAPTER TWENTY-TWO

When Twilight showed him the letter from David Trask, Cooper became angry as the meaning of the words registered.

"What does he mean you don't have title? You've lived there all your life."

"I don't know what it means. I don't understand."

"Well, I'll call Billy Adams. He'll know what to do about this."

Cooper looked up the number and dialed. Billy's secretary explained that the attorney was in court, but she expected him in the office after lunch. She would be sure to give him the message.

"Twi, if you don't mind I'll keep the letter until I talk with him?"

She handed him the envelope, as well.

Billy returned the call later in the day. After exchanging greetings and small talk, Cooper got to the point. After he read the letter the older man exploded.

"That Duh . . . David Trask is a goddamned disgrace to the profession. I'm amazed he hasn't been disbarred. Most of his clients are nothin' but thieves. One of 'em, Mark Long, was involved in that mess over at Shell Point when that old couple got dispossessed. That bunch are worse than snakes."

"Mark Long?" Cooper asked, "wasn't he in charge of sales over at *Ocean Dunes*?"

"That's him. He left Jenkins and struck out on his own. He specializes is small to medium sized condo projects. He's a slippery bastard. Give me Twilight's legal address and I'll make some calls. I got a friend who knows a lot more than I do about heirs' property, and if you like I'll respond to Trask."

"We'd appreciate that. Thanks for your help, Billy."

"My pleasure. Give your uncle my regards."

Billy called back two days later. "Cooper, I found out more than I wanted to know. We need to discuss this situation. I know you can't travel just yet, so I'll just come and see you. I can't remember the last time I had a day out of the office. Besides, it'll give me a chance to catch up with Henry."

When Billy arrived on Friday he spent well over an hour at lunch with Henry before they both rode a cart over to Cooper's place. Billy was noticeably impressed with the big house.

"Jesus, this is great. Look at that view."

With the help of his crutches, Cooper led them to the shaded deck where they found seats facing each other. Billy looked older but his mannerisms hadn't changed. His eyes still had a wide-open look of amazement, but somehow his stuttering did not seem quite so apparent. He wore a flamboyant bowtie, as always, and his shirt and suit were neatly pressed.

The three helped themselves to iced tea from a pitcher on the table. Billy drained half a glass before he launched into a tirade.

"Cooper, this whole heirs' property mess stinks to hell, but the problem goes way back. In 1831 a well-educated slave named Nat Turner started a rebellion up in Virginia. They put it down real quick, but not before fifty-five whites were slaughtered. Whites all over the country were scared to death they might be next. They blamed Turner's education for the uprising, so they enacted legislation here that made it illegal to teach blacks to read or write."

Billy had another sip of tea. "Thirty five years later, after the war between the states, General Sherman made outright gifts of property to former slaves here and in southeast Georgia. But a couple of years after that, President Johnson rescinded the grants and returned the property to its former owners. Well, without slave labor they couldn't turn a profit. Most of 'em bailed out. Freedmen started buying up the land cheap, or worked it off as sharecroppers."

Cooper offered more tea, but his guests declined. Henry unwrapped a cigar but did not light up.

Billy continued. "Now remember, the first generation of black landowners couldn't read or write, but most of 'em knew enough to have someone else draw up a will for them. Their heirs have no problem. But the families of the ones who died intestate are in a real fix. Their land is owned jointly by all their living relatives. There can be as many as thirty or forty. Any one of them can petition the court to sell the property at a partition sale. Okay, what if a long forgotten cousin is down on his luck, or just doesn't give a damn about a few acres he's never seen? That son of a bitch Long or someone like him can buy his partial interest for a song and then get the court to order a sale. It's nothin' but thu . . . thievery, but in this case the thievery is legal and it's sanctioned by the state."

"These days the land is worth a hell of a lot more than it was back then, especially water oriented parcels. Now that we've got modern drainage techniques, air conditioning and mosquito control, you can build luxury condos on what used to be bottom land. So you've got developers lined up at partition sales with more money in their pockets than the heirs will see in a lifetime."

"What compounds the problem is that most of the victims are poor blacks. They don't trust lawyers who are mostly white, and if the lawyers aren't stealing their land, they don't want to get involved in heir's property cases because they're time-consuming and unprofitable."

"Wow," said Cooper. "You learned all that since just the other day?"

"Well, the more I dug into it, the more pissed off I got. It makes me ashamed of my profession."

"What about that letter?" Cooper asked.

"I think that was just a fishing expedition, you know, to see if Twilight would tumble for the fifty thousand. I've done a little research and it appears that she is the sole heir to that property. I guess her great-grandfather's people were not very prolific breeders, but just to be on the safe side, I'll respond to Trask. I'll let him and his cronies know that if her land is ever put up for sale, there would be no point in them trying to outbid you."

"By the way, I almost forgot. David Trask has him an errand boy. It seems Deputy Sonny Fletcher, is working for him on the side."

Henry had been listening intently. "You know, it just occurred to me, Twilight's place is tucked in between the Ashley tract and the old Bell property. The Bell place is for sale and I heard the Ashley property sold a couple of months ago. If the same person got hold of all three pieces, he'd have him a right big chunk of riverfront real estate."

Cooper displayed a quizzical expression. "I wonder if something like that happened to Sally Timms' land on Dolphin Island. She was Twilight's grandmother. Twilight would take me to visit when I was little, and I went with her to Sally's funeral. Soon after that the court ordered a sale and a developer came up with the winning bid. It's pretty land, probably ten or twelve acres and right on the water. It's part of *Pelican Cove Resort* now."

"When did that happen?" asked Billy.

"A year or so after she died. I remember Twilight telling me about it."

"Well, what's done is done. No point in rehashing that."

"I know. It's just that everyone was surprised when she passed suddenly like that. She was old, but she was happy and healthy."

"How did she die?" asked Billy.

"In her sleep, I guess. A friend from church went to check on her when she didn't show up for a prayer meeting."

"Did anyone notify the coroner?"

"The undertaker over there doubles as the coroner. He ruled it a natural death."

"How old was she?" asked Billy.

"No one knows for sure, but Twilight thinks late seventies or so."

Billy stood up and looked out at the ocean. "I remember when they were starting that *Calibogue Creek* place over there. The developers built a damn sales office right smack on a Gullah cemetery. It's possible they didn't know it at first because the old black cemeteries had no head stones. But the Gullah people damn sure let 'em know. Even so, they wouldn't tear it down or move it. That's when things got a little ugly. They called names back and forth and finally the Gullahs called in Dr. Lizard to do something about it.

"Who's Dr. Lizard?" asked Cooper.

"You mean who was Dr. Lizard. He's dead now. He was a root doctor from over near Frogmore. He had a clientele that stretched from North Carolina down to Florida, and west damn near to Atlanta. Had a huge reputation. If he put the whammy on you, you'd have a hell of a time finding someone to take it off."

"At any rate Lizard took a ferry over there one day and surveyed the situation. He saw the sales office sittin' on the cemetery then he did his thing with potions or crows feet or whatever, and he put a root on the developers so they could never make any money on that island."

"From what I hear, they never made a penny. And that's not all. That other place, the one with the private ferry system should have been built out long ago, but they've got less than half the homes that were planned. The folks who own them get hit with huge assessments every year for the amenities, but they can't sell 'cause no one wants to buy and be saddled with the extra fees."

"What do you think will happen?" Cooper asked.

"Beats me, but unless they come up with someone with more mojo, I wouldn't bet against Dr. Lizard. Well, I need to be on that afternoon boat so I'd best be going. Talk with Twilight, Cooper, and let me know how you want me to proceed."

CHAPTER TWENTY-THREE

An emotional reunion took place two weeks later when Kathleen arrived for a visit. Wanda and Twilight had not seen her since her family's departure from the island. There were hugs and kisses and tears, but finally Cooper wrested her away. He couldn't wait to show her the house on the beach. He ushered her to his cart and deposited her small suitcase in the back. In minutes they were parked in the sandy driveway at the base of the stairs. He pointed out the lift and explained how Simon had designed and constructed it. She was in awe.

"My God, this place is huge. When did you build it?"

Cooper related how he and Peter Wilson had collaborated on the plans, but he let it go at that.

"Let's go on up. It's got a great view of the beach. I'll take your bag but I'm afraid you'll have to walk." He stepped onto the lift and ascended as she mounted the stairs. They reached the top at the same time.

"Okay, now close your eyes. Put your hand on my shoulder and follow me." Cooper opened the door and grasped his crutches before leading her to the center of the floor. "Now open your eyes."

Kathleen put her hand to her mouth. "Oh Cooper, this is beautiful." She turned and noticed the balcony in front of the second floor bedrooms. She turned again and looked out the wall of sliding doors to the beach. Cooper opened one and beckoned her out onto the deck. She was speechless.

The water sparkled in the afternoon sunlight. Several small fishing boats bobbed at anchor on the shoal that ran parallel to the inlet. Birds filled the sky as the sea breeze billowed through the chintz curtains next to the opened door.

"This is our beach, Kat. There's the tree where you posed for my sketch, do you remember?"

Kathleen stepped outside and let the sea air fill her lungs. She said nothing for a moment, but when she turned towards him there were tears in her eyes.

"Yes, I remember, but it all seems so long ago." She moved towards him and they embraced.

"I love you Kat, I want to be with you forever. Will you marry me?"

"Oh Cooper, I've guess I've always loved you but I need more time to think. I just need to sort everything out."

"Fair enough, but let's get you settled. If I could, I'd give you my room and take one of the others but I can't manage the stairs quite yet. I hope you don't mind."

"Of course not, I'll go up now. I'd like to freshen up a little."

"Okay. We're going over to Uncle Henry's for dinner. We should be there at six or so."

"Do we have time for a quick swim?"

"Sure, I'll meet you on the beach."

Cooper looked totally out of place standing at the water's edge supported by his crutches. He turned to see Kathleen approaching in her bathing suit. Her figure looked as trim as he remembered, and she still looked very beautiful. Her eyes just seemed a little older. He reached down and picked up a sand dollar.

"Here, think you can skip it five times?"

She laughed and sent the disc skimming along the tops of the small waves. It hopped twice before vanishing.

"Not bad, not bad."

"I'm a little out of practice," she laughed.

"Well, let's go in. It's supposed to be good for my legs."

They waded through the surf until they could swim. Then Cooper let go of his crutches and they plunged together into the warm water. They splashed each other, laughed and giggled like kids, and each thought of their days together so many years ago.

After half an hour Kathleen retrieved the crutches, and they left the water together. They stopped at a pair of outdoor showers near the back stairs where they rinsed away the salt. Each grabbed a fluffy towel from a weatherproof locker.

"Oh Lord, it's almost five-thirty. We'll have to hurry."

"You go ahead, Kat. I brought my clothes down so I'll dress here. I'll meet you at the cart when you're ready."

They arrived as Henry watered his flowers out front. Ettie sat in a rocker on the porch, and a spark of recognition flashed in her eyes when she saw Kathleen. She stood and displayed her doll, and Kathleen gave her a hug.

Melanie had fixed flounder almondine with new potatoes in a dill sauce and a salad of greens with slices of fresh tomatoes. An embroidered linen cloth covered the table, and she had laid out her best silver for the occasion. A centerpiece of roses added an elegant touch, and there were wine glasses at each place but Ettie's.

Uncle Henry opened a bottle of cold Chablis and moved around the table pouring. Cooper turned his glass over, "thanks no, I'll just have water."

Catching up on the intervening years kept the conversation lively until nine-thirty, and because Kathleen insisted on helping to clear the table, they did not leave until ten. Back at the house Cooper stepped out of the lift as Kathleen reached the top of the stairs. He opened the door and ushered her in.

She asked, "I noticed you didn't have any wine. Don't you like it?"

"Kat, I had a talk with Jake Bennett at the hospital. He thinks I have a problem with alcohol, and he might be right. I told him that I planned to ask you to marry me, and that I would promise that I'd never have another drink."

"Oh Cooper, that's sweet."

"Kat I won't push you. I know you need more time. But no matter how long it takes, I'll be here waiting for you."

She came to him and kissed him. "Thank you for understanding. I knew you would." She traced the scar on his forehead with her finger and kissed him again before going up the stairs.

Cooper was already asleep when her movement woke him. He could just make out her form coming towards him. She lifted the sheet and got in beside him. He felt her warm skin next to his as she put her lips to his ear and whispered, "Cooper, I have always loved you."

They had been apart for years, but their excitement surpassed that of the day years ago when they first explored each other's bodies. Now, for the first time they coupled, softly and slowly, so as not to hurt his legs. She murmured, as they climaxed together. She kissed him hungrily as tears ran down her cheeks. They were starved for each other, and hours later when they finally drifted off they were locked in an embrace.

In the morning they made love again before making their way to the beach. Naked under the robes they shed in the sand, they entered the water together as the waves caressed them.

"Kathleen, in the light of day and with the majesty of the ocean all around us, I ask again. Will you be my wife?"

Kathleen began to cry. Her shoulders heaved. "There's something you don't know about me. I had his baby."

Cooper blurted, "Baby? Whose baby?"

"His, Sonny Fletcher's."

Comprehension crept into his expression. "But how? I didn't think it went that far."

"Neither did I. You and I had never done it, so I didn't know. I thought it took longer. It went on for only a minute or so before you got there."

Cooper was dumbstruck. The significance of what she said hit him like a blow to the gut. He turned away, but she had seen the look in his eyes—not hatred, something worse. She had seen revulsion.

Kathleen sobbed. "That's why we moved away. My parents found out I was pregnant. They wouldn't believe me about the rape. They thought it was you."

Cooper stared out at the horizon, his mind trying to make sense of her words. He thought about that night all those years ago, and the four figures struggling on the ground in the near dark. He recalled Sonny Fletcher cowering in the dirt and he wished he had killed him. He remembered covering Kathleen's nakedness with his T-shirt and the look in her eyes as he took her home.

He turned abruptly. "What happened to the baby?"

"Adopted. My parents arranged it with the church."

"A boy or a girl?"

"They kept it away from me but one of the nurses told me I'd had a girl."

Cooper kept silent. He made his way back to the beach as Kathleen followed. They both donned their robes and walked to the house.

Kathleen got ready to leave. She had duty at the hospital that night. After she packed her things, Cooper drove her to the Landing in silence. Wanda intercepted them and hugged Kathleen before they all walked down to the dock. Cooper and Kathleen came together for a stiff embrace but his eyes conveyed dismay. As the boat pulled away Kathleen waved but they could see that she was crying. When the boat pulled out of sight they turned and started up the ramp.

"Wan, you knew about the baby didn't you?"

"Yeah, I knew. Kathleen smuggled out a letter and told me about it. Her parents shut her in and wouldn't let her talk to no one."

"What happened to it? The baby I mean."

"They took it from her the day she had it."

"Has she ever seen it?"

"Cooper, she don't have no idea where that child is. The records are sealed by the court so she can't never find out. Every time she tries to get some information she runs into a dead end."

Wanda fixed him with her blue eyes, "That don't change the way you feel about her, does it?"

"I don't know. I just don't know. If only it was someone else, and not Fletcher."

"Let me tell you something Mister. That girl ain't done nothing mean or nasty her whole life. She didn't want to get raped, and she didn't ask for the hard-hearted parents she got neither. She's had a full share of tough luck and none of it's her doin'. If you can't understand that, you ain't the man I thought you growed up to be."

Cooper didn't respond. He limped to a table and sat alone, looking over the creek. Wanda left him and went back inside.

He sat there for a good half hour before he made his way to the dock. Minutes later he steered a skiff across the Sound to the marina at *Ocean Dunes*. He took a seat at an outside table at the *Flying Fish* and glanced at the menu.

A waitress appeared. "The special today is grouper melt on a bun with fries and slaw. It's real good."

"That sounds good but I'd like a Bloody Mary first, and make it a double please."

Cooper sat hunched over the table with both hands wrapped around the drink. His mind replayed the image of Kathleen lying half naked in the dirt with Sonny Fletcher on top of her. He gulped the rest of the drink. He had two more before the waitress asked again if he would like to order.

"Okay, I'll have the special, and while we're at it I've had enough of these," he held up the empty glass. "Bring me a Jack Daniels on the rocks, water on the side please."

Jeannie's battered face next flashed in his thoughts. The drinks were taking hold and he began to grit his teeth. When the waitress served his meal he ordered another bourbon. She could see he was getting drunk, and she alerted her manager who peeked outside. Cooper had barely touched his sandwich. He turned his head, waiting impatiently for his fresh drink.

"I think that's Cooper Hamilton. He used to come in here all the time. I haven't seen him in years."

She reached for the phone and dialed a number from the list on the wall.

A woman's voice answered, "Hello, *Dis'n'Dat.*"

"Hey Wanda, it's Ginny over at the *Flying Fish*. We've got a customer who's pretty plastered, especially for this time of day. He looks like Cooper Hamilton. Could it be him?"

"Oh shit. Yeah, that's him. He left here a few hours ago in the skiff. Is he causin' any trouble?"

"No, the place is practically empty. I'm just worried about him getting back across the sound."

"Thanks Ginny, I'll have someone come over and carry him home."

When Simon arrived, Cooper had passed out at the table. His crutches were on the ground next to him. Simon shook him but he just mumbled. Simon tried again with the same result before pulling Cooper upright and hefting him over his shoulder. He crossed to the dock and placed his dead weight in a seat on the crab boat he'd borrowed. Simon went back for the crutches and stepped inside.

"Does he owe you anything?" he asked Ginny.

"Nope. We put it on his American Express. Here, you better take this. We don't want someone else to walk off with it." She handed Simon the card.

He thanked her and retrieved the crutches before walking to the dock. He took the bow line from the skiff and tied it off before piloting both boats back across the sound. Simon reversed the procedure at the Landing, carrying Cooper up the ramp and across the deck to an empty cart. He propped him up and slid in next to him holding his collar with one hand and driving with the other. At the house, Simon deposited his burden in the lift and pushed the up button. He had already reached the top of the stairs when the car bumped to a stop. He opened the door and manhandled Cooper to his room where he dumped him onto the bed.

After pouring some tea from the refrigerator, Simon slid open a door to the deck and sat back in a rocker. He dozed off for a while but Cooper's voice woke him.

"Is anyone here? Can anyone hear me?"

Simon ignored him.

A few minutes later he heard it again. "I have to go to the john. I can't find my crutches. Can someone help me?"

Simon sat up and walked to Cooper's door.

"I'm gonna be sick. Can you help me to the bathroom?"

"Well now, you didn't ask for help to run off and get drunk. Seems to me you did that all by yourself. So get yourself to the bathroom."

"But I can't find my crutches."

"You got more crutches than anyone else I know. You're just a little candy ass."

Cooper looked at him in astonishment, his bloodshot eyes focusing on the big man. "The hell with you, I'll do it myself."

He eased himself to the floor and crawled to the bathroom where he pulled himself up to the commode. Simon watched him open the lid before he started back to the great room. He heard coughing and gagging and the sound of the toilet flushing, followed by silence.

Simon stayed on the deck until the last rays of the sun disappeared behind the pines and palmettos. He went back to Cooper's room and saw him curled up in a fetal position on the still-made bed. Simon left him alone and went to fix something to eat. After another hour on the deck, he rummaged around for a blanket before stretching out on one of the big couches in the great room.

The rising sun woke him in the morning, and he switched on the coffee maker. After it perked he took a steaming mug to Cooper's room and put it on the nightstand. He opened the drapes wide, and sunlight flooded the bedroom. "Okay party boy, it's time to rise and shine."

Simon shook Cooper's shoulder. He heard a groan and then a few seconds of silence followed by a grunt. "Oh shit, I've got a headache."

"Well that's a good sign. Maybe you aren't brain dead after all. There's some coffee on the table there. You better drink it. We've got work to do today."

"Where did you come from?"

"I brought you home after you passed out."

"I guess I ought to thank you."

"You ought to thank Wanda and Twilight. I would have left your sorry ass over there, but they talked me into going after you. The Cooper I thought I knew would never have sent that girl home crying, and he wouldn't have crawled back into the bottle after promising he was through with the stuff."

"You don't understand. She had that basterd's baby."

"You think she made that choice? Do you think she asked to roll around in the dirt with those bums? You need to get real Cooper. Getting raped has nothing to do with who that girl is. What makes you so perfect?"

Cooper turned away. "I was . . . just shocked."

"Well, Twilight was shocked when you went on a bender. She believed in you."

"I made a mistake, I'm sorry."

"Yeah, you are sorry, but maybe down deep there is something worth saving. We'll see, but now we're going to work."

Simon handed Cooper his crutches. "Let's go."

"Where are we going?"

"We're going swimming. Get into your trunks."

Simon had reached the bottom of the stairs when the lift bumped to a stop. "Follow me," he grunted. He led the way to the beach. Leave your crutches here and put your hand on my shoulder. Simon led the way into the surf.

"One of the best things for your legs is swimming. It builds up the muscles with minimal impact on your joints. Let's see if you can make it to the point."

"You're not serious. I can't go that far."

"Well if you can't I'll have to carry you like a baby. But I always thought you were a pretty rugged guy."

Cooper shot Simon a cold glance but said nothing. He plunged into the water and started off towards the point. Simon followed fifteen yards behind, prodding him, "You can kick harder than that. Use those legs. Work the muscles."

After twenty minutes, Cooper's pace had not faltered. He might have stopped to rest since the water was only waist deep but he kept going, doggedly raising one weary leg after the other.

Simon admired his grit. He pulled abreast of Cooper. "Why don't we take a little break?"

Cooper continued to pull.

"Don't you want to rest for a minute?" Simon asked again.

Cooper spit a mouthful of water. "I'll rest when I get to the point."

Simon dropped back and followed him for another fifteen minutes until they reached the sand spit at the south end of the island. Cooper swam into shallower water and sat on the bottom kneading his shoulders and arms with his hands.

"You keep that up and you'll be a hundred percent in no time," said Simon.

Cooper flashed a weak smile before he doubled over and retched. After he had emptied the meager contents of his stomach his expression softened. "I didn't think I could do it. Thanks for pushing me."

"Why don't you rest for a while? I'll run back and get a cart."

"I can make it back on my own."

Simon looked concerned, "You don't want to overdo it. You'll be stiff tomorrow as it is."

"I can make it. I'll just take it a little easier."

Cooper looked directly at the big man. "Simon, I feel like a real asshole about yesterday. I'm sorry you had to come get me. I owe you a lot, but I wonder if you would do me one more favor."

"What's that?" Simon asked.

"Will you drive me to Macon? There are two people I've really got to see."

"Well, I've got two days before my next trip. Mind if I ask who the second one is?"

"Jake Bennett, he's the doctor who saved my life. He's also a drunk like me, but he belongs to a support group. I need to find out more about it. And I've got to see Kathleen. I need to make her understand that I love her no matter what."

Simon put his hand on Cooper's shoulder. "Why don't you find out where her little girl is? That way she'd know you mean it."

Cooper sat silently for a moment, staring into Simon's eyes. "You know what? That's a great idea, and I know someone who might be able to help."

They borrowed the keys to Henry's mainland car and took the skiff to Bluffton. The drive to Macon took just under three hours. They found Jake's apartment with no trouble and it was just past six-thirty when Cooper stepped out of the car. Simon would be back for him in two hours. Jake answered the door with a smile and a handshake, but did not invite him in.

"Come on. There's something I want you to see." He led Coop to his pickup.

"Where are we going?" asked Cooper.

"I want you to meet my support group."

In less than ten minutes they were parked at the side of a long, low building that served as a conference center for the local electric utility. Others were arriving, and Jake greeted several of them as they all entered an open door. Folding chairs were set up in rows. They found two together not far from the speaker's podium. People around them chatted amicably until an attractive woman approached the podium and leaned into the microphone.

"Hello everyone, and welcome. Let's get started. My name is Miriam, and I am an alcoholic. It has been six years since I had my last drink."

Cooper could not take his eyes off her. She was well-dressed, attractive, and obviously in good health. She looked to be in her mid-thirties, but a hint of something in her eyes made her seem older. He wondered why she would say such a thing.

Miriam continued. "Starting off this evening, we're going to hear from one of our newer members. He is celebrating five months of sobriety. Please welcome Bob."

Everyone applauded as a handsome man stepped forward to the podium. He appeared to be forty or forty-five. He wore a business suit and looked hale, and his dark hair was beginning to gray at the temples. He glanced around at the twenty or so members before beginning.

"Good evening. My name is Bob. I am an alcoholic. I have been sober for one hundred and fifty-four days, thanks to God and to you, my friends. I have learned from my visits here that my experience is not unusual, but it is uniquely mine, and I will share it with you in hopes that some of you may find a common thread that will help with your own healing."

"I got my first real job right out of college. I sold cars at a Ford dealership in Atlanta. In less than six months I became the top sales producer. In three years I worked my way up to assistant sales manager. Then I met the love of my life. A year later, I asked her to be my bride. After our marriage, I became sales manager and assistant general manager."

"Life could not have been better. Soon we had two wonderful kids, first a boy, and then a girl. We bought a home in a great neighborhood where we made many good friends and we entertained or were entertained just about every weekend. I never thought about it at the time, but alcohol played a major part in all of our socializing."

Once we hosted a big party to celebrate our tenth anniversary. I got very drunk, and I had a blackout for the first time. I couldn't remember anything the next morning."

He went on to describe the series of events that took him to rock bottom. He began to arrive late for work, and started to sneak shots of vodka to help him through his frequent hangovers. After being warned twice, he was fired for losing a deal with a fleet customer. Bob dismissed his former boss as a fool and hired on at a competing dealership across town.

But he suffered a big cut in income. The bills began to stack up, and his wife had to find a job. When he was fired again, less than six months later, his wife began to carp about his drinking. He claimed it relaxed him, but she contended he had a problem. Their arguments became bitter. They fell behind on the mortgage payments and had to put the house up for sale.

It was a sad story. Cooper could sense the pain of the man at the podium. He could see the anguish in his eyes.

"I had lost everything including my wife. My own parents wanted nothing to do with me, and I had not seen my kids in three years. I moved down here to Macon, and I lived on the street like an animal. I could not sink any deeper. Then one day, without a friend or a nickel to my name, I noticed some people coming in here. They greeted each other like family. I waited outside for a while before I sneaked in the side door. That's when I heard another man tell a story much like mine."

There were tears in Bob's eyes as he finished, and everyone in the room thought back to the defining moment in their own lives that had brought them to this place.

Bob got another round of applause, and several people stepped forward to shake his hand.

Jake reached for Cooper's arm. "What did you think?"

"These are just regular people like us. I guess I expected to see bums."

"That's a common misconception. We are real, everyday people, and we try to help each other stay that way."

"I can see where this would be great for me, but it's a little far to come."

"I've done some checking," said Jake. "There's a group that meets in Savannah. I'll give you the address."

Kathleen sat alone at the chart rack with her back to him when Cooper stepped off the elevator. He had made it halfway across the floor when she turned. Surprise filled her eyes. He extended a huge bouquet of roses, "I must be the world's biggest jerk. Kat, don't say anything, just listen for a minute. I came to tell you that I love you. I know I can never be happy without you. I am ashamed that I reacted the way I did about the baby. It was a shock. But I'm over it, and it will never come between us again. Please accept my apology. I don't expect you to give me an answer now, but I'm begging you to give me another chance."

She said nothing. She stood facing him holding the roses with an expression of surprise in her eyes. He turned and hobbled to the elevator on his crutches.

Kathleen found her voice. "Where are you going?"

"Back home. Simon's downstairs waiting."

Tears filled her eyes. "Oh Cooper, will you call me tomorrow?"

He turned, "tomorrow and the day after, and the day after that. I never want to spend another day without you."

She ran to him and embraced him. As the elevator doors opened she kissed him. "Oh Cooper, I love you so."

CHAPTER TWENTY-FOUR

His legs were stronger now. Whether they were swimming or walking, Simon constantly prodded him to go faster and farther. When he cramped up Simon massaged the bunched up muscles until they relaxed.

On a warm morning Simon appeared at Cooper's front door. "Okay, today is the day. No more crutches."

Simon bounded down the steps as Cooper rode the lift. "You just walk behind me and put one hand on my shoulder. Today we're going for two miles."

They started off on the dirt path but after just a few steps, Cooper removed his hand and continued on his own. His progress was slow but he managed to keep going.

"Man, that's great. You've been holding out on me," said Simon.

"I worked out some while you were gone this time."

"You're making real progress, now. We'll be jogging before long."

Cooper laughed. "Wouldn't that be something? By the way I asked a friend to keep his eyes open for a good, clean boat. He called me yesterday. There's a thirty-five foot Viking for sale at *Ocean Dunes*. She's a late model with twin Cats and low hours. Maybe we should run over and take a look?"

"Viking's a great boat. They raise fish and do well in the tournaments. When do you want to go?"

"We could go later on today if you have the time."

"Sure. That's fine with me."

It was love at first sight. *Different Drummer* glistened as sunlight danced on her waxed hull and topsides. She had obviously been well maintained. The owner, Troy Holcomb, stepped out of the salon and they all shook hands.

Cooper could not conceal his admiration, "She looks new."

"I've tried my best to keep her that way. I bought her two years ago and took delivery at the plant up in New Jersey. Just a few months later I learned I had colon cancer. I went through surgery and chemotherapy, but a month ago they found more cancer. This time I've got to have a full colectomy. I can't keep her up any more. I just don't have the heart for it."

Cooper felt a pang of sympathy for him. He could tell that the man loved his boat.

"I've opened the hatches so you can see everything. The generator's on the centerline forward."

"Take a look, Simon," Cooper gestured. He explained to Troy about his legs. "I don't think I'd better crawl down in there just yet."

Simon lowered himself into the engine room between the bright yellow Caterpillar engines. The space was clean, and he could find no trace of rust.

"These hoses and clamps all look new," he said.

'They are. I replace 'em every year," said Troy. "You can't be too careful, especially below the water line."

Impressed, Simon climbed back out as Holcomb led them forward to the single stateroom. He pointed out the head and shower to port, and the galley to starboard. Everything looked brand new.

"Let me show you the flybridge."

They followed him up the brushed aluminum ladder to the helm. The complement of electronics included radar, Loran-C, auto pilot and radios, all in good working condition. She had double-spreader Rupp outriggers and teaser reels mounted on the hardtop supports. She was a fishing machine.

Troy lifted the seat cushion off a storage box and displayed four 50 lb. and two 80 lb. rod and reel outfits. They were Penn Internationals, the best available. "I won't have much use for these I guess, so they'll go with the boat."

Cooper sat on one of the two seats behind the helm. "Troy, we can see the boat is in great shape. We're definitely interested. How much are you asking."

"Let me say this. Who I sell her to means as much to me as how much I sell her for. How do you fellows plan to use her?"

Cooper swiveled his seat so he faced the older man.

"We both love to fish. Simon mated for years on a sport boat in the Abacos. I grew up around here and started fishing with my uncle as soon as I could walk. We're no strangers to blue water. I think I know how you feel about your boat. She's like a member of the family. I can assure you we'll take good care of her."

"I'm sure you will. Let's go below."

They followed Troy down the ladder and sat on the L-shaped couch in the air-conditioned salon. After handing Simon a beer and Cooper a coke, Troy opened a beer for himself. He took a small scratch pad from a drawer, jotted down a figure, and handed it to Cooper. Cooper noted the amount and passed the pad across the table to Simon. They locked eyes for a second as Simon nodded imperceptibly.

Cooper extended his hand. "That's a fair price, Troy. You've got a deal."

They shook hands all around, and after drawing up a simple sales contract, Cooper wrote a check for ten percent of the amount. They would return the next day for a sea trial. If there were no surprises, Cooper would render the balance.

"Troy, if you don't mind we'll bring along a friend. He's a great fisherman and a licensed surveyor. We'll need the survey in order to get insurance."

"Of course. I guess the sooner we finalize this, the better. Otherwise I might change my mind."

Next day the sea trial revealed no surprises. *Different Drummer* performed flawlessly. She cruised at an honest twenty-four knots at 2,400 RPM's, and all her systems were in good order. When they hauled her out at Palmetto Bay Marina, her bottom was clean, freshly painted, and free of blistering. The shafts were true and the props had no dings or dents. Neil Bender considered it the easiest survey he had ever conducted. Troy shook Cooper's hand and wished him good luck. Cooper could see that the experience pained the man.

"Troy, any time you feel like wetting a line, give us a holler. We'd be glad to have you."

"Why thank you, Cooper, I will."

But they all knew he never would.

Different Drummer became a permanent fixture at the Landing. Cooper made the rounds on Hilton Head to let other captains know she would be available for charters when the regular boats were all busy. On average she had charters two days a week, and whenever Simon had a break he came along as mate.

Cooper still had plenty of time for his work. He began to concentrate on wildlife and seascapes. His paintings took on new dimensions and became bolder. They found a ready market at the high-end galleries in Charleston and Savannah.

On rare occasions he appeared at showings, although he believed most of the clients they attracted were there to be seen themselves, not to admire the art. He found the events tedious, and invented excuses why he could not attend. Unwittingly his attitude may have added to his works' appeal and helped to create an aura of mystery about the elusive artist.

Whenever Simon had the time they would go fishing. It might be a charter, or just the two of them running out to the artificial reefs or the Navy training towers off the Georgia coast—easily reached on a one day jaunt. The structures held bait that attracted amberjacks, king mackerel and cobia. Sometimes mahi mahi would make an appearance. On fewer occasions they fished the Gulf Stream. The Stream harbored trophy-sized wahoo and billfish, but at seventy-five miles offshore the round trip plus five or six hours of actual fishing made for a long day. If time allowed they would go out for two days, spending the night on board.

They perfected their techniques, but they knew they would need more hands to compete successfully in tournaments. After long deliberation they offered berths to Neil Bender and Tyler Merrill, seasoned anglers whose experience complimented their own.

Simon had reservations about Tyler. "He can be a hothead. Three days is a long time to be around someone with a short fuse."

Cooper countered, "I say we give him a chance. He's a hell of a fisherman, and if he acts up, well, we'll just find someone else."

Tyler caused no problems and fit in well as the crew honed their skills during the first year. They became a precision team.

Each had a very specific assignment. As captain, Cooper piloted the boat. The ability to out-maneuver or back down on a big marlin was critical. He had to gather information about tides, weather, and sea temperature, and decide where to fish.

Simon handled the rod. As the biggest and most powerful of the four, he could endure a physical contest with a great fish that might last for hours. Tournament rules were strict. No one else could put a hand on the rod.

Neil was the wire man. He had a solid build, blonde hair and steel-blue eyes. With a fish on he would swivel the fighting chair so Simon always faced the quarry, but when Simon angled the fish close to the boat Neil would grab the leader with a gloved hand. He had to know just when to let go if too much tension threatened to part the line.

Tyler served as third mate. He was tall and thin with long brown hair gathered in a ponytail. Tattoos covered both of his arms. Tyler inspected the gear, replaced any worn or chafed line, and rigged the baits. He also wielded the all-important gaff hook.

It amounted to tough, exacting, and spilt-second teamwork, but the crew of *Different Drummer* earned a reputation as formidable competitors on the circuit.

During a big tournament out of Georgetown, foul weather forced a cancellation on the first of the three days. The seas were still roiled on the second day, but eighteen of the twenty-six boats ventured offshore. Two crews had hookups, but neither could bring their fish to gaff. Day three started out with a brisk twenty-five knot blow out of the Southeast. Most of the crews threw in the towel, but eight contenders remained in the hunt. Cooper and his crew decided to fish half the day. If nothing developed by noon they would head for home.

They trolled a variety of teasers, lures and live baits for several hours with no result. Then at 10:45 the radio crackled with news of a potential winning fish. *Salt Shaker*, out of Charleston, had boated an estimated four-hundred fifty pound blue. The wind had laid down to just 10 to 15 knots, so with a little over an hour to go until their self-imposed deadline the crew of *Different Drummer* decided to go for broke.

Simon rigged a garbage can lid on a length of quarter inch line and secured it to a cleat with shock cord. He tossed it overboard as Cooper and Tyler reeled in the other teasers. When the slack disappeared from the line, the lid dove and zigzagged, popping in and out of the water, creating a commotion both above and below the surface. All eyes were on the spread where two flat line and two outrigger baits skipped along on the faces of waves in the wake.

Five minutes passed, then ten. Suddenly, Cooper bellowed from the bridge, "starboard rigger, starboard rigger."

The thrashing lid had raised a big marlin. From its size, Cooper guessed it was a female. Precision bedlam ensued as the men jumped to their stations. Simon took his seat in the chair and snatched up the rod. As Tyler reached for the line to pull in the metal lid, a swipe from a huge bill sent it flying towards the boat. The big fish changed directions abruptly and made a beeline towards the other outrigger bait.

"Port rigger, port rigger," screamed Cooper. "Christ she's huge, and she's lit up like a Christmas tree."

The brilliant colors of the fish, triggered by territorial instinct and evolutionary magic pulsed like flashing neon. Simon jammed the rod into its holder and picked up the one opposite. He switched off the drag and held the rod tip high in anticipation.

Cooper shouted, "Here she comes. Easy, easy…"

Line began to spool off the reel but Simon counted to ten before he engaged the drag.

"Now," he shouted.

Simon heaved back on the rod as Cooper rammed the throttles forward. The boat lurched ahead momentarily in order to help set the hook then settled back as Cooper shifted to neutral.

"Have we got her?" he shouted from the bridge.

Simon could do nothing but watch as line screeched from the reel.

"Oh yeah," he responded.

The fish breached the surface three times, tail-walking and shaking its head in an attempt to lose the hook. Simon held the rod tip high in order to keep tension on the line. Then she went deep. The ensuing battle lasted three hours. Muscles rippled in Simon's back and shoulders as he pumped the rod up and down. Each time he regained a precious foot or two of line and brought the quarry closer to the boat. Every few minutes Neil hosed Simon's head and bare shoulders with cool fresh water and squirted the reel to keep the drag from overheating.

When Simon finally wrestled the fish close to the boat Neil grabbed the leader and led it to the port side. Tyler stood ready with the gaff but all he could see was one huge, malevolent black eye before the fish lunged. With a swipe of its tail, it catapulted away from the boat. Neil dropped the leader as the marlin streaked towards the horizon again.

"Oh, man," griped Simon. "I thought we had her. What time is it?" His body glistened with sweat.

"Two thirty," Cooper responded.

"Damn," Simon said to himself as he began to recapture the lost line.

The fight continued for another fifty minutes before Neil could reach the leader again. Cooper backed down hard in order to shorten the distance. Following seas cascaded over the transom, flooding the cockpit with a foot of seawater, but the prize came within reach again. Neil had the leader in hand and led the exhausted fish to the port side where Tyler stood ready with the gaff.

"Wait, wait!" gasped Simon holding his hand up to stop him. "What time is it?"

Cooper, looking down from the bridge, glanced at his watch. "It's three twenty-three."

"How far out are we?" asked Simon.

Cooper checked the instruments. "We're right at forty-four miles from the inlet."

No one said a word as all four men realized there was little chance of getting back by the five p.m. deadline.

"We'll never make it. I say we let her go," Simon said quietly.

"Are you crazy?" Tyler glared at him in disbelief.

"There is no point in killing the fish if we can't make it back in time," Simon said.

Cooper looked down at his crew. "Okay, we'll vote on it. Who wants to release?"

It took several seconds for them to weigh that option against the possibility of sharing in the eighty-six thousand dollar purse.

Tyler spoke first. "No way. There's a lot of money ridin' on this and I could use it. Let's land her and bust ass back in."

Neil echoed him. "This is the first time we've had a chance to score big. Cooper, check again. There must be some way we can make it back in time."

"I could use the money too," said Simon, "but there's no sense killing a trophy just for bragging rights. We can't make it on time. Let's face the facts."

Tyler glared at him. "What the hell do you know? Who put you in charge?"

Cooper interjected. "Listen up. We're forty-four miles out. At top speed we run twenty-eight. That means we might reach the inlet at 4:59. We'll still have two miles to the dock. Let's vote. Who wants to cut her loose?"

Tyler looked at each of the others. "Are you guys crazy, it's just a goddamn fish. We've still got a chance."

"I'm for release," said Cooper.

"Release," said Simon.

"Neil?" Cooper looked down from the bridge.

"Ah shit. Let's let her go."

"Sorry Tyler," said Cooper, it's three to one. Cut the line.

"You cut the goddamn line."

The others looked at him, astonished. Not one had ever before exhibited mutinous behavior.

"I'll do it." Neil pulled a pair of wire cutters from his pocket and reached over the side to part the leader. The beautiful colors had dimmed and the once fierce expression in the big eyes was now one of resignation. The huge tail swiped slowly as the big fish disappeared into the depths. It looked every bit of eight hundred pounds.

Tyler sat silently on the gunwale. He took the beer Neil offered without a word but kept his eyes on Simon. Simon and Neil climbed up to the bridge with a coke for Cooper and cold Coronas for themselves, but Tyler refused to join them. Without him they toasted each other all around and settled in for the long run home.

Simon reflected, "It's a damn shame. The long liners are raping the seas. Every year there will be fewer fish. If we don't do something about it, sport fishing will be just a memory. Tournaments should be release only."

"How would they keep them honest?" asked Neil.

Cooper answered, "Simple. Just put an observer aboard every boat."

When they neared the marina at *Ocean Dunes*, Simon and Neil climbed down from the bridge. Tyler was drunk. Empty beer cans littered the cockpit. He stayed in the fighting chair and didn't make a move to help. After the lines were secured Tyler rose with his sea bag in hand and stepped ashore. He stood unsteadily on the dock and looked back at the others.

"I've had it with you jerks. You can find yourselves another deckie. I'm gonna sign on with a crew that knows how to win." He walked off.

Neil bunched his fists and started after him, but Simon grabbed his arm. "Don't waste your energy. It's not worth it."

"I don't believe that guy, what an asshole." Neil gathered his things and shook hands with Cooper and Simon. "Next time, guys. Next time."

Simon loosed the lines as *Different Drummer* eased away from the dock. They rode in silence back to Spanish Island.

CHAPTER TWENTY-FIVE

Cindy returned from the kitchen to find Cooper perched on his regular stool at the Racquet Club. "Hi, Cooper, we've sure missed you. I'm so sorry about your accident. I hope you're feeling better."

"Thanks, Cindy. I'm doing much better. It's good to see your pretty face."

She blushed, "Thanks, what can I get for you?"

"I think I'll wait. I'm just here to see Dawson."

"He should be in any time now. He'll be glad to see you."

As if on cue, the attorney made his appearance. He wore a navy suit with a white shirt and a conservative striped tie. He looked the part.

"Well, well, old chum, I've been thinking about you. I've missed you. Cindy, the drinks are on me. I'll have the usual. Cooper, what'll it be?"

"Just a Coke on the rocks."

Dawson arched an eyebrow.

"I quit drinking, Dawson. I nearly killed myself in that accident. I'm a drunk. A friend hooked me up with a support group in Savannah that helps me stay sober."

"Well I'm happy for you, but I mourn the loss of my old drinking buddy."

"I'm moving back home permanently. I'm doing some work that I'm really excited about, and for once I'll have time to do some serious fishing."

"How boring!"

"You city boys will never understand."

They shared a laugh.

"Dawson, I'm here to ask a big favor."

Cooper related the old story of Kathleen's rape. He was honest about his reaction to the news of the baby and the fact that it had triggered a drunken binge.

"I reacted badly. I'll never forget seeing her in tears when she left that day. I have to make up for that. I have to prove to her that I'm over it. I don't ever want it to come between us again."

Dawson swiveled his stool to face Cooper. "Well, what can I do?"

"They took the baby from her at delivery and put it up for adoption. She knows it's a girl, but that's it. She has tried to find out where the child is, but she keeps running into dead ends. The court sealed the records."

"Well, go on."

"You once told me that you had a contact on the Georgia high court, a family friend as I recall. Would you be willing to ask for his help to get some information about the child?

"Jesus, old pal, that's a large order."

"I know it is, but there's no other way. Kathleen is totally blameless, and she would give anything to know something about the child. I didn't tell her I'm doing this because I didn't want to get her hopes up."

"Cooper, the court seals records in these cases to protect the child, as well as the adoptive parents?"

"I know that."

"Birth mothers are curious creatures. Years later pangs of conscience can surface. After all, blood is thicker than water. But unfortunately, when natural mothers are reconnected with adopted children the result can be heartache for all concerned."

"Dawson, Kathleen would be satisfied just knowing the child is well and happy."

"Where was it born?"

"In Georgia. Milledgeville."

"How old would she be now?"

"Let's see, I guess about thirteen."

"That's a tough one Cooper. A girl of that age is impressionable. It would be terrible to turn her world upside down, particularly if she doesn't know she's adopted. Want another coke?"

"Sure. Okay.

Dawson gestured to Cindy.

Cooper continued, "Okay, how about this? Let's say I retain you to find out what you can with the understanding that you would not have to give me her name, or identify her parents, or reveal where she lives."

"What would that accomplish?"

"At least we'd have some answers. Then, let's say I set up a fund to pay for her college education with no strings attached."

"They could take the money and that would be the end of it."

"They could. As I said before, Kathleen would be happy to know that the child is in a loving home. She doesn't expect to meet her or share in her life."

"Old buddy, you're talking about putting out a substantial pile of dough for nothing but a little information. As your friend and former counselor, allow me to say I think you're out of your goddamn mind?"

"Listen Dawson, I showed up when they were raping Kathleen. I stopped it. She was a virgin and had no experience. It lasted just a minute, and neither of us thought anything had really happened, but I guess I arrived a little late."

"What ever happened to the rapist?"

"He's still in the area. He's a deputy sheriff believe it or not. Sometimes I wish I had killed him. I just want Kathleen to have some closure about this thing. She knows she can't have the child, but it's hers. I guess it's only natural she'd care about it. It's not a selfish thing. She would be content just to know the girl is okay."

"Are you telling me that you will risk that much money just to learn if the child is healthy and happy?"

"Yes. However, as my representative, I'd like you to leave the door open for any opportunity to meet with the parents, and or the girl, if and when they want. That's not a condition, just an invitation."

"My friend, if it means that much to you, I'll give it my best shot."

"Dawson, you're a prince."

"I'll need all the details you can get; mother's full name, date of birth, name of the hospital and so on. By the way how long will you be in town?"

"Just a few days. I'm cleaning out my office at the agency and selling the furniture out of my apartment. I found someone to sublet beginning next week."

"Well okay, why don't we meet here day after tomorrow?"

"Sure. Maybe we can have dinner as well."

"Old chum, it will take me a while to get used to the new you."

CHAPTER TWENTY-SIX

Cooper and Kathleen were married in late September on the beach in front of the house. A pastor from Bluffton officiated. The day might have been specially ordered by God. With hair flying in the breeze, Cooper kissed his bride against the backdrop of the sea as gulls wheeled above the waves. Boats full of curiosity seekers, anchored just off the beach, blew their horns as the band launched into its first number. The couple walked hand in hand to the temporary dance floor.

Somewhat ungracefully, Cooper led his bride to the strains of Elvis' *The Wonder of You*. At the last note, with all the guests on their feet clapping and whistling, Kathleen's eyes welled as Cooper bowed before her. She was radiant. Her floor-length dress of pale ivory organza fell off her bare shoulders while lustrous auburn hair framed her face and her incredible blue eyes. A single diamond graced each of her lobes.

"Kathleen, I will never love anything or anyone as I love you. You make me whole. You are the center of my life. He straightened up, held her close, and kissed away her tears as the band broke into *Old Time Rock and Roll*. Guests flocked to the dance floor.

Everyone from the Spanish Island showed up along with many guests from other islands and the mainland. Kids ran and played around the perimeter as old friends held spirited conversations at one of the bars set up at two locations around the pool. The locals were dressed in their Sunday finest. A riot of color complimented the natural beauty of the setting. Extravagant beds of begonias, impatiens, marigolds and hibiscus added a finishing touch.

A popular restaurant from Savannah catered the affair. Uniformed waitresses served everyone at decorated tables under the big tent on the lawn. As the newlyweds made the rounds, Cooper noticed Gwen and Dawson Spruill together on the dance floor. Kathleen had been right about seating them together, and Rick Bennett could not keep his eyes off one of Kathleen's friends from Macon. It was a glorious affair, but because of logistics it had to wind down at 10:30. All available boats would be at the Landing at 11:00 to transfer guests to the mainland. Kathleen held Cooper's arm as she and her new husband bid goodbye to their friends.

They would leave early the next day for Atlanta where they would catch a flight to San Francisco. Long ago Cooper had promised that he would show Kathleen the beauty of coastal California. He had not forgotten.

After a long day traveling, they spent their first night at the Mark Hopkins. Kathleen thrilled at the pulse of San Francisco and the magnificent views of the city and the bay. She marveled at the elegant Nob Hill shops and boutiques but refused Cooper's offer to buy her a diamond bracelet as a memento.

They spent three days in the city before driving south to Monterey where they visited the Language School and Old Fisherman's Wharf. They had drinks and toasted John Steinbeck at Cannery Row before dining at The Mission Ranch over the mountain in Carmel.

The couple spent several days exploring Pebble Beach and the Carmel Valley before driving down Highway One through Big Sur to San Simeon. They stopped at remote and deserted beaches and enjoyed lazy lunches at picturesque stops along the way. Every night they stayed at a different inn. Each seemed more intimate than the others. Kathleen drank in the beauty of the rugged coast. She could not wait to get up and go each morning, but not before their easy and prolonged intimacy.

After showering one morning she peered at her image in the mirror. She looked as happy as she felt. She could not be more in love. But something nagged at her thoughts. She wanted to go home. As much as she enjoyed visiting California, she wanted to be back on Spanish Island where they would start their new life together. She had to know it was real and not just a fairy tale. It would seem so only back at Cooper's house on the beach, in Cooper's bed, with Cooper beside her.

On their last morning after making love he asked, "Are you sure you want to go home? We can stay here forever if you like."

She nuzzled his ear and rolled closer to him. "I can't wait to get home."

"We've got a stop to make on the way."

"Where?"

"Nashville."

"Nashville? In Tennessee?"

"Yup."

"What's there?"

"Someone we need to meet."

"Well, who?"

"Sorry, it's a surprise."

Kathleen hit him with a pillow. "Tell me who?"

"Okay, okay."

Cooper got out of bed and crossed the room. He pulled a small manila envelope from his carry-on bag and extracted a five by seven color photo. He produced a picture of a young girl with pretty blue eyes and light brown hair. She smiled, and the braces on her teeth sparkled in the light of the flash.

"I'd like to introduce you to your daughter."

Kathleen was stunned. "Where did you get this," she asked never taking her eyes from the image.

"I asked Dawson Spruill to do a little checking for us."

Kathleen could hardly speak. "Wha . . . what's her name?"

"It's Meridith."

"She's very pretty isn't she?"

"I think she's beautiful, like her mother."

Kathleen showered and fixed her hair mechanically, her mind never straying from the idea that she would meet her daughter, her own flesh and blood, the very next day. Somehow she had managed to pack her things and pull herself together before it was time to leave for the airport. She bombarded Cooper with questions that he couldn't answer.

Finally he held his hands up in mock defense. "Look, Honey I really don't know any more than you do. Wanda told me you had tried to find out about your daughter. She said you reached a dead end because the court had sealed the records. I knew that Dawson had a contact on the Georgia high court, and I thought if anyone could get some information, he might. Well, it turns out he hit a home run. I couldn't believe it when he called back to say the Gibsons were eager to meet us."

"When did he tell you that?"

"He called a week or so before the wedding. That's when I changed our itinerary."

"Well what did he say about them?"

"According to Dawson, they sound very nice. Rocky, that's the husband, leads a country-western band. Evidently, he does very well."

"Will they think I abandoned my own child?"

"Honey, Dawson explained everything to them. They know you had no choice in the matter."

It had been a long day. Their flight to Chicago arrived an hour late and they almost missed the connection to Nashville. When they checked in at The Hermitage, the desk clerk handed them a note in a flowered envelope. It was addressed in a woman's hand to Mr. and Mrs. Cooper Hamilton.

Dear Folks,

Welcome to Nashville. We hope you had an easy trip. We're all excited that we'll be meeting you tomorrow. Rocky and I hope you will come have lunch with us at the farm. It will be simple and much more relaxed than a restaurant. We hope that works for you. A map is enclosed, but we are easy to find, and not more than a half hour from The Hermitage. Unless we hear from you otherwise, we will look forward to seeing you at noon.

Sandi Gibson

"How nice," Kathleen said. "I like her already." She was physically and emotionally exhausted. She undressed quickly, brushed her teeth and dropped off as soon as her head hit the pillow. But she was wide awake three hours later. She stared at the ceiling as she tried to decide what to wear. What would be the first words she would say to her daughter? How could she explain the emptiness she had felt for so long not knowing a thing about her only child?

Except for fitful catnaps, she was awake the rest of the night. But when Cooper stirred at seven, Kathleen had dropped into a deep slumber. He did not disturb her, but dressed and went to the lobby in search of a newspaper and a cup of coffee. When he returned after half an hour he found her crying and pacing the floor.

"I'm so nervous. Maybe we should just go home and leave everything as is."

Cooper embraced her. "Honey, everything will be fine. Jump in the shower and I'll order breakfast. How about eggs benedict?"

She nodded and smiled through her tears.

The Gibson's farm nestled in the rolling hills west of town. Split rail fencing lined the long drive leading up to the main house. Fall was in the air. The leaves on the trees were crimson and gold and the grass in the pasture was the color of oatmeal. Two horses watched as Cooper and Kathleen stepped out of their rental car. A pretty, plump woman waved from the front door and walked towards them. Sandi had dark hair, brown eyes, and wore a simple blouse and skirt. She looked to be in her middle forties.

"Hi Kathleen, I'm Sandi." She extended her hand first, then hugged her guest. "I am so glad you're here."

She turned to Cooper and shook his hand with a smile.

"Meri's as nervous as can be. We've talked about this day for years, and the day has finally arrived."

"How did you know . . . ?" Cooper started to ask.

"We've been doing some checking on our own. It would have been just a matter of time until we connected with Kathleen, but you beat us to it. Come in, come in."

The big moment was over in an instant. Meridith sat quietly on a couch when they entered the big, sunny front room, but on impulse she jumped up and ran to Kathleen. The two embraced and both broke into tears. In seconds they were deep in conversation.

Sandi took Cooper's arm and ushered him into another room. "Let's leave them alone for a few minutes."

In the study, a balding, non-descript man sat in front of a piano with a large set of earphones covering both sides of his head. He stood up when they came in, removed the headset and extended his hand. "Hi, I'm Rocky Gibson. Welcome, welcome."

Rocky looked to be about fifty. When Dawson told him the man was a musician in Nashville, Cooper expected him to look like Kenny Rogers or Johnny Cash. Rocky did not come close.

He gestured to a stuffed chair. "Have a seat."

As the two men engaged in small talk, Sandi discovered that something needed her attention in the kitchen. It smelled wonderful.

Cooper explained his recent departure from advertising and learned that Rocky had worked with several Atlanta ad agencies. They even had a few mutual acquaintances. The man was relaxed and genuine.

"We do a fair amount of commercials, but mostly we record musical sound tracks for movies and TV shows. How about something to drink? A cold beer, maybe?"

"No thanks, but I'll have a Coke if you're having something."

Rocky filled two tumblers with cubes from a small icemaker and poured Coke over the rocks. He handed one to Cooper. "Cheers."

"Good health," Cooper responded.

"You know, we had been trying to get a line on Kathleen for several years when your friend called us. It came as a pleasant shock. Sandi was adopted and never could learn anything at all about her birth mother. When we discovered she couldn't conceive we decided to adopt, as well."

"Four or five years ago Sandi became determined to track down Meri's natural mom. She didn't want the girl to go through life just wondering as she had. We've been honest with her from the beginning. We've never hidden a thing from her. She knows she is adopted and she is happy and well-adjusted."

Cooper glanced out the big window and caught a glimpse of his wife and Meridith standing next to a fence. The girl was stroking the nose of a chestnut mare and looking up at Kathleen. He turned back to Rocky.

"She's turned out to be quite a young lady."

"All it takes is love. All it ever takes is love."

Cooper looked squarely at the other man. "May I ask you something personal?"

"Well, sure. Go ahead."

"When I first approached Dawson about helping to find Kathleen's daughter, I didn't think her adoptive parents would agree to a meeting. I assumed that the appearance of the natural mother after all these years would be considered intrusive. But you folks have opened your arms to us. I'm overwhelmed."

"Well, let me say this. We are all totally comfortable about the love we have for each other. Nothing can ever change that. When Mr. Spruill called us and mentioned your offer to pay for Meri's college tuition, we knew that your intentions were honorable. We have already provided for Meri's education but it was nice to know that her birth mother had no ulterior motives."

"Well," Cooper raised his glass, "I admire you."

Sandi's voice came through the open door. "Okay you two. Lunch is served. Come and get it."

Rocky drained his Coke and set the glass down. "Cooper, let me ask you something."

"Sure, go ahead."

"Would either of you have any information about Meri's real father? His name maybe?"

The question caught Cooper by surprise. It had never occurred to him that the Gibson's might also be curious about the natural father. After a long pause he heard himself say, "I thought you knew. Kathleen was raped."

"Oh, I'm sorry.

"Come on boys," called Sandi.

Rocky stood up. "We'd better get in there."

They sat around a huge farm table in a bright, airy room with views of fenced pastures outside the windows. A fresh green salad with tomatoes and onions sat at each place. Sandi passed a platter of fresh rolls and poured sweet tea from a frosty pitcher. The conversation flowed easily. Kathleen was no longer nervous, and she and Meri laughed and chatted like old friends. She could not take her eyes off the girl.

After the salad, Sandi disappeared into the kitchen. She returned with a tray of individual cottage pies, and by the time they finished the meal they were all comfortable with each other. Kathleen and Meri helped to clear the table as Sandi produced a freshly-baked peach pie.

They stayed at the table long afterwards until Cooper and Kathleen had to leave. They had all agreed that the Gibsons would visit Spanish Island in the spring. Meri had never seen the ocean, and Kathleen promised to show her how to catch big, blue-claw crabs with just a piece of string and a chicken neck.

As they were leaving, Sandi presented Kathleen with a wrapped gift after extracting her promise not to open it until she was home. Cooper drove down the long drive as their hosts waved from the front of the house.

Kathleen looked over at her husband. "I don't know how to thank you. You can't imagine how hard it's been not having any idea. Thank you from the bottom of my heart."

"Honey, I've got to tell you something. When we were alone Rocky asked if I knew anything about Meri's father. I didn't lie. I just told him that you were raped."

"What did he say to that?"

"Nothing. I guess he figured that we didn't know who did it."

"Maybe that's the best thing."

Cooper shook his head. "Something's bothering me. They never kept anything from Meri. Maybe we should be up front too. She has a right to know who her natural father is."

Kathleen sat in silence for a few moments. She turned and looked out the window, struggling with her feelings.

Cooper continued, "Look Honey, it's not something we have to decide right now. We'll have plenty of time to talk it over before they come in May."

After a light supper in the lobby, they went up to their room for the night. Kathleen was emotionally exhausted. She fell asleep quickly but woke after a couple of hours. She could not contain her curiosity about the gift. She slipped out of bed and opened the package and found a photo album. Inside she found a note from Sandi.

Dear Kathleen,

I've always known that someday we would locate Meri's birth mother, so whenever we took photos I had extra copies made. This is your record of her progress from the time she first came into our lives. I hope you will cherish it as I do mine.

Love, Sandi

Kathleen was in tears again. Sandi's magnanimous gesture had moved her deeply. She leafed through the pages again until she had examined every image. As she glanced at her sleeping husband she thought back to his reaction when she first told him about the baby. She understood how he must have felt, yet he had overcome his feelings to make this day possible. No one could ever make her happier than she felt at this minute.

CHAPTER TWENTY-SEVEN

On a Wednesday afternoon Cooper and Simon had just dropped off a charter at *Ocean Dunes* and neared the Landing when Simon pointed and shouted, "I don't believe it. There's *Alibi,* the boat I fished in Abaco." He pointed at a sport fisherman tied up at the fuel dock. "What in the world is she doing here?"

As soon as they tied up, Simon hurried to the other boat. He knocked on the salon door but got no response. He sprinted up the ramp and arrived at Wanda's just as Robert Culmer stepped out the door. The two men embraced in a bear hug.

"It's so good to see you Cap'n Robert."

"You too Simon. I've missed you."

They sat at one of the tables on the deck.

"You look well, Cap'n. How is Mrs. Culmer?"

"She's having more trouble with her hips, and I expect we'll have to get her a wheel chair before long. We're neither of us getting any younger. My knees bother me more these days. I can't get up and down the stair to the bridge like I used to. I've retired. I sold *Alibi* to a man in North Carolina."

"She looks as good as the last time I saw her."

"Well, you kept her in top condition, and I've tried to do the same. The trouble is I could never find anyone who is half the mate you were."

"You're very kind Cap'n"

"Simon, I mean it. You're a professional. I hope they appreciate you here."

"We sure do." Cooper came up the ramp. "Sorry, but I couldn't help overhearing."

Simon introduced the two.

"I've heard a lot about you Robert. You're a legend."

"Well, I've slowed down considerably, but we had some good years didn't we Simon?"

"Yes sir. We sure did."

As they spoke, a young black man came out of Wanda's and watched them intently before proceeding down the ramp. Robert called after him. "Nelson, this would be a good time to have a look at that hydraulic problem."

"Yes, sir," came the muted response.

"Well, I'll leave you two to catch up on old times," said Cooper. "How long will you be with us Robert?"

"We'll be pushing off in the morning."

"In that case why don't you come over for supper this evening? It won't be fancy but it will be filling.

"That's kind of you, but I wouldn't want to intrude."

"Any friend of Simon's is a friend of ours. Besides I'd like to learn more about your fishing techniques."

Robert smiled. "In that case, I'll look forward to it."

"Good. Simon, why don't you and Twilight bring Robert over at six."

Cooper waved and strode through the door to say hello to Wanda. She sat at her customary place behind the counter. He leaned over and gave her a peck on the cheek before extracting a cold Coke from the cooler.

"That man asked a lot of questions," she said. "Who is he?"

"That's Robert Culmer. Simon fished with him in the Bahamas."

"Well he sounds like Simon, his accent I mean. What's he doing here?"

"He sold his boat. He's on his way to deliver it to the new owner."

A customer unloaded a small basket of purchases as Cooper fished a couple of quarters out of his pocket and put them the counter. "Got to go Wan, see you later."

Simon and Robert remained at the outside table catching up. Robert produced a letter from Simon's mother who hoped he would visit before long. She and Mary were well, but they missed him and were anxious to see him.

"I hope I can visit them soon," he said, as much to himself as to Robert.

"Well, Simon, who is Twilight?"

"She's a friend. She's a few years older but we really like each other. She practically raised Cooper." Simon explained about Ettie's condition and suddenly exclaimed, "There she is now."

Robert turned to see a small, pretty woman walking towards the front of the building. Her white hair was neatly brushed and held back by a comb with a yellow bow. She wore a bright sun dress and had the figure and appearance of an adult, but her movements were childlike. She held her head erect and looked straight forward as if on a mission. She cradled a little blond doll in her arms.

"She comes here every afternoon. She acts as though she's never seen the place before. Wanda fusses over her and pours some iced tea. She'll have a few sips and pretend to give some to the doll. Then she'll walk some more. She wanders all over this end of the island but everyone looks out for her. She's never in any danger."

Robert watched until she disappeared from view. "What a tragic thing. Can't she say anything?"

"She doesn't speak at all, but she's always making dolls. That's how she expresses herself. Twilight communicates with her somehow. I don't understand it, but I think it's something like telepathy."

"Well, Simon, you look fit and happy. Life here must agree with you."

"I enjoy my life here Cap'n, but I miss working with you. I mate for Cooper when he has a charter, and sometimes we'll go out just for the fun of it. I wish you could meet Henry, but he's shrimping down in Georgia this week."

"Captain Culmer," called Nelson coming up the ramp. "Can you come look at the steering pump?" His eyes never left Simon.

"I'll be right there, Nelson. Well, I guess we'll have to continue this later. What time shall I meet you?"

"We'll pick you up at six, said Simon."

"Does it take long to get there?"

"No, we could walk it in five minutes but Twilight has a cart so we'll ride."

"Does Cooper smoke cigars?" asked Robert.

"No, why?"

"I've got some Cuban cigars aboard if you think he might enjoy them."

"I don't think so, but if you tell him they're for Henry it would mean just as much to him."

The sea breeze had cooled the air to seventy-eight degrees when the three stepped from the cart onto the sandy path that served as Cooper's driveway.

The big house appeared to be three stories tall, but the living area perched atop a system of pilings, raising it eighteen feet above the sand, and twelve feet above the hundred-year storm surge elevation called for in the county building code. Three sides of the ground level were sheathed in painted lattice providing shaded parking for vehicles and storage for bikes and other outdoor equipment.

As they mounted the stairs they were greeted with a cheery, "Here they are now."

Cooper swung open the screened door and ushered them inside. The kitchen, dining and living areas shared the same huge space with unfettered views of the beach. Glass panels and sliders looked out over the covered deck that spanned the ocean side of the house.

"Come in, come in."

Kathleen wiped her hands on her apron. She wore sandals, shorts, and a colorful blouse

"Honey, this is Robert Culmer," said Cooper. "You've heard Simon talk about him."

"Of course. Hello Robert, I'm Kathleen. It's so nice to meet you."

Her smile was natural as a flower and the tiny wrinkles at the corners of her eyes only made it more appealing.

"Please come in. We'll sit on the deck? The breeze is wonderful this time of day. Cooper, if you'll make everyone comfortable I'll be there in a minute. We're having Lowcountry boil and I've got to check the sausage. Robert, would you like a drink? Twilight and I are having red wine."

"Why a scotch on the rocks would be nice if you have it."

"Sure we do. Cooper, would you mind? I'll pour the wine."

Cooper fixed a drink for Robert and opened a Corona for Simon. He poured coke over ice in a glass for himself.

Robert said, "Cooper, you've a lovely spot here, and your home is beautiful. I understand you designed it."

"Well thank you, I helped. An old friend who's an architect did most of the work."

"By the way, I'm not familiar with Lowcountry boil. It sounds very good, but what is it?"

"It's just another way to serve shrimp," Kathleen laughed. "Actually, it's quite good. It's a combination of fresh, unpeeled shrimp, chunks of sausage, quartered new potatoes and corn on the cob. It's all simmered together with salt, pepper and special spices. I hope you'll like it."

"I'm sure it will be delicious."

They sat at a round table on the deck. Kathleen ladled generous portions from a steaming tureen into brightly colored chowder bowls at each place. Squares of corn bread, fresh from an iron skillet, were heaped on another plate. The shrimp were caught just hours earlier. Cooper picked them up from Ben before coming home. The breeze off the ocean stoked their appetites, and everyone had their fill.

"That was delicious, Kathleen. Cooper is a lucky man."

She winked, "Thank you, Robert, but it took me a while to get his undivided attention."

Kathleen and Twilight cleared the table and returned with a tin of hot apple crisp and a bowl of vanilla ice cream. Everyone groaned, but no one refused a portion.

Robert said, "By the way Cooper, I brought a little something." He handed the package across the table. "These are from Cuba. Simon tells me that you don't smoke but I thought your uncle might like them. He's the one that rescued Simon. It's the least I can do."

Cooper unwrapped the package, "Wow, Cohibas! Thank you, Robert. Uncle Henry will love these. But while we're on the subject, I've always wondered what happened to Simon out there. Simon, is it so bad that you can't share that with us?"

Simon cast a sidelong glance at Twilight and then at Robert. "Okay, I owe that to you."

They all listened as he related his story of the high-jacking of *Abaco Belle*.

Simon departed Marsh Harbor at eight a.m. enroute to Ft. Lauderdale. He made good time during the day. The wind was light from the southeast, so the Gulf Stream crossing would be easy. When he rounded West End at sunset his chart showed the Ft. Lauderdale sea buoy at sixty-nine nautical miles to the southwest on a bearing of 243 degrees. Simon came around to a course of 228, fifteen degrees further to the south, in order to compensate for the northerly set of the Stream's current. He switched on the autopilot and ducked below to brew some coffee. He had brought his own since the galley cabinets and forward cabin were empty except for two bulging, olive-drab duffle bags stuffed under the berths. They were marked *Diving Gear*—standard equipment for a lobster boat, but oddly each was padlocked. Simon thought it strange that Marley had forgotten to give him the keys.

As the coffee brewed, he went topside and scanned the horizon. He saw no lights but he heard a deep rumble to the east. There moon had not yet risen, and only blackness lay behind him beyond the glow of his lights. He shrugged and went below to fill his mug.

He had returned to the helm when he heard the noise again. Now, it sounded more like a guttural roar. The other craft was coming fast, but he still could not see it.

Minutes later a searchlight flooded his helm with brilliance, temporarily blinding him. Involuntarily he swiveled towards it. While keeping the light in his eyes, the other boat pulled abeam and a voice ordered him to heave to. Simon complied because he had no idea what else to do.

"What were you thinking?" asked Cooper.

"I didn't know what to think. I thought it might be Air/Sea Rescue."

As Simon watched, the other boat came along side, and two men jumped aboard. One carried a baseball bat.

"Okay boy, where's the merchandise?" one asked.

"Merchandise? What are you talking about? I didn't take anything."

The bat caught him on the left side of his face. Simon heard the cartilage snap in his nose and felt blinding pain shoot up the side of his head. Enraged, he lunged at the man, knocking him to his knees. As Simon flailed with his fists hoping to connect with the man's face, the second man moved behind him and felled him with a blow to the base of his neck. Simon crumpled to the deck as the first man continued to work him over.

"Go look for the coke."

Satisfied that Simon would not jump right up, the second man went to take a look below.

In a minute he burst back on deck. "Holy shit, Ramon, it's right up forward in a couple of duffel bags."

"Well get it out here. Hurry up."

When Simon stirred, Ramon approached him again with the bat. As he did, Simon launched a kick at the man's leg and connected with his knee He must have done some damage because Ramon bellowed in pain, stumbling across the deck where he dropped to a sitting position.

He glared at Simon and hissed "I'll fix your black ass." He pulled a switchblade from his pocket and flicked it open. Getting back to his feet he started across the deck.

Simon could not believe what was happening, but he'd heard stories of high-jackings and modern-day pirates boarding vessels and killing the crew. He had to get off the boat.

The man had come within three feet of him when Simon sprang to his feet and vaulted over the side. Ramon bellowed, and the second man appeared from below and produced a gun. Bullets streaked into the water around him as Simon swam under the hull and forward towards the bow where he could not be seen.

He poked his head up long enough to hear Ramon say. "Forget him. He's bleeding, and the sharks will get him soon enough. Get the stuff into our boat."

Simon reasoned he could hide next to the bow, and, if necessary dive underneath until they had gone. He would then find some way to get back aboard and continue on to Ft. Lauderdale.

That's when he heard Ramon say, "Put the charge right over the fuel tank."

They were going to blow up the boat. In a rush of panic Simon realized that if he were close enough, the concussion would kill him. Without another thought he took a deep breath and swam underwater, away from the two boats. Silently popping up after a couple of minutes, he allowed only his face to appear above the surface. After gulping his fill of air he went under again, swimming with all of his strength.

When he heard the other boat's engines accelerating he surfaced again and watched it speed off towards the west. Now the running lights burned brightly. A minute later he saw the explosion. Bits and pieces of *Abaco Belle* shot skyward as he heard the blast. Seconds later he felt the concussion, but he was far enough away and, for the moment, still alive.

He could not help wondering how it would be to drown. He could hold his breath for two minutes or so, but what would happen next? Would his lungs gulp seawater? Would the gag reflex make him cough and trigger the involuntarily inhalation of more water? Would he continue to breathe until his oxygen starved brain shut down his organs? Would he lose consciousness quickly, or would awareness linger as he sank slowly into the depths?

As he watched, flames reached into the air. He wondered if the blaze could be seen at West End, but quickly calculated that it was too far to the east. He noticed something big and bulky bobbing in the light of the flames and recognized it as one of the large deck coolers. He swam to it with all his strength.

While he never really slept, he drifted in and out of a daze. He was cold, very cold. Even the warm waters of the Gulf Stream are well below the body's normal temperature. Simon tried to climb inside the cooler, but each time it would flop over and fill with water. He finally learned to straddle it, a tactic which kept most of his torso above the surface. He watched helplessly as the lights of at least six ships appeared and then disappeared from sight. None came within a mile of his position.

He tried not to think of the bizarre events of a few hours ago. He had to concentrate on staying alive. But his mind would not cooperate. He realized that he had been duped into delivering a load of drugs. He had been caught in the middle but had no idea how or why. Did the buyer double cross Marley, or had he been high-jacked by freelancers who found out about the deal? In any case, who would believe that the boat had been blown up, the drugs stolen, and that he was still alive? For all anyone would know, *Abaco Belle* had simply disappeared.

He made it through the night, and the soft light of the dawning day cheered him a bit. He had mastered the technique of straddling the cooler and staying on top. He made himself believe he would be rescued.

He must have dozed off for a few minutes when something brushed by his leg with enough force to knock him back into the water. He watched, shaken, as a dorsal fin turned back towards him. He took a breath and slipped below the surface. A tiger shark came at him, but he delivered a kick to the creature's snout and drove it off temporarily. He suddenly realized that blood from his face covered his shirt. He tore it off and rolled it into a tight ball before throwing it as far as he could. When it hit the water with a small splash, the beast circled to investigate. Signaled by some primordial stimulus, it lunged and swallowed the shirt and disappeared with one sleeve trailing from its jaws.

"Oh, my God, how horrible," Kathleen said, her hands to her face.

For the next hour and a half, Simon spent most of his time under water. In order to defend himself, he had to see the shark coming. As long as he could kick or punch, it would break off. But if he became passive, it would be all over. He grew weaker by the minute. His arms and legs started to cramp, and he knew he could not hold on much longer.

He had almost slipped beneath the surface for the last time when a boat hook caught him by his arm. He looked up and saw a big, white man looking down at him from a fishing boat. Another man climbed down a rope ladder and helped him aboard.

"That's how it happened. I still have no idea who did it, but your uncle saved my life, and you all know the rest." Simon took a deep breath.

CHAPTER TWENTY-EIGHT

When Robert Culmer's mate, Nelson, returned to Abaco, he went straight to Lucas Marley. Nelson knew about the reward for information on Simon's whereabouts, and he planned to claim it. He told Marley about the stopover at Spanish Island and Simon's reunion with Culmer. Marley was now convinced that Simon had made off with *Abaco Belle* and the drugs she carried. High-jackers would have killed him. Why else would he not return home? Marley meant to claim his pound of flesh.

In less than a week, he set off for South Carolina. He would have to be shrewd and patient, but he would make an example of Simon Albury, and no one would ever try to steal from him again.

On a brisk morning in late October, Cooper had just finished fueling *Different Drummer*, when a sleek powerboat transited Spanish Creek, turning port into the channel to the Landing. She looked to be thirty-eight or forty feet in length. Powerful engines rumbled and sunlight glinted off her black hull. Cooper replaced the fuel cap and strode down the dock to offer a hand. A black man with bulging eyes threw him the bow line. Cooper tied it off before repeating the process with the stern line. The captain was a bald white man with a bushy beard. Cooper wondered how he could have so much hair on his face and none on his head. The two strangers surveyed the dock and the marina, and nothing seemed to escape their scrutiny.

"Need some fuel?" Cooper asked.

"Yes, diesel," grunted the white man, jumping onto the dock. He towered over the other man and had an athletic physique.

"I just finished. I'll clear the pump and switch it on for you."

"What's up there?" the man asked pointing up the ramp.

"*Dis'n'Dat.* It's a convenience store, but everyone calls it Wanda's. She sells sandwiches and hamburgers and she's got a bar if you're thirsty. When you finish pumping, you pay for your fuel up there."

Cooper returned to his boat. He hosed down the cover board where a few drops of diesel had escaped and dabbed the water droplets with a towel before polishing the surface with a chamois. There would be no spots on *Different Drummer*.

He walked into the store and watched Wanda struggle with a new device she called a personal computer.

"Hi, Sweetie, come over here and give old Wanda a hug."

"I just pumped some fuel, but I'm afraid to ask what I owe you," he said producing an American Express card.

"Bullshit. You know you get the family discount. If I hadn't got roped into that so many years ago, I'd be retired by now. How you doin' Hon? I mean really?"

"Wan, I haven't had a drop in over fourteen months. I really don't miss it, but it's funny, every once in a while it sort of pops into my head like an old friend, like right out of the blue. I just have to remind myself that it's one old friend who's dead and gone."

"We're all real proud of you, Sweetie."

Wanda finished with Cooper's transaction just as the bearded man came through the door. His eyes took in everything. "How much for the fuel?"

Wanda checked the computer screen that showed the number of gallons he had pumped. She touched a few more keys, and a white tape spewed out the top of another machine to her right. "That'll be a hundred sixty two, seventy."

The man produced a pair of hundred dollar bills. "How far is Savannah from here?"

"About twelve miles."

She handed him his change and a receipt along with a mimeographed chart of the local waters. "Take a left at the green marker about three hundred yards up the creek and follow the Intracoastal the rest of the way."

He grunted and looked around once more before leaving.

"Real friendly isn't he?" said Cooper.

"I've seen 'em all in this place."

Cooper leaned on the counter, "How's Karl?"

"He's got his good days and his bad days. But it's gettin' harder to tell which is which."

"Is he getting around okay, I mean with his wheel chair and all?"

"Pretty much, but he won't even try the damn crutches. It's like he's content to be an invalid. And he won't quit drinkin' or smokin'. You'd think anyone who lost a damn leg would wise up, but not Karl."

"He's been at it a long time. I don't think I'd recognize him without a Lucky in his lips and a Bud in his thermos."

"You got that right."

Cooper pulled an icy Coke from the freezer and put a dollar on the counter. Wanda pushed his money back and took a quarter from the cash register. "Here go play D-14 for me, Honey." The music of The Eagles soon filled the otherwise quiet space.

After reconnoitering Spanish Island, Marley realized he would need some local knowledge. Instead of turning south for Savannah, he followed the chart to Hilton Head where he tied up at the marina at Palmetto Bay. Later that afternoon he left his mate with the boat and went to explore the shops and restaurants adjacent to the marina. At *Captain Woody's* he found a seat at the bar and ordered the first of several beers. Marley watched the comings and goings of several patrons before two men came in and sat near him. He listened to their conversation until he was satisfied they were locals. He bought them a round of drinks and introduced himself. Their names were Craig Wellons and Jimmy Sykes and they were native to the area.

His plans for Simon would require accomplices who wouldn't flinch at crossing the lawful line. He had to know if they would pass muster. Marley bought another round of drinks and asked if they knew where he might buy some marijuana.

"How much you want?" asked Wellons.

"Three or four ounces ought to do it."

"I can have it for you tomorrow."

These were his boys. They were not a threat, and they would probably jump at the chance to make a few thousand dollars.

"Okay. Are the police a problem in this area?"

"We ain't got police, we got deputies," Sykes blurted, "and the deputy in charge is our buddy."

"Shut up, Jimmy," said Wellons, but Marley had caught what he said.

Marley explained that he was a businessman and that an associate had stolen some merchandise that belonged to him. He had tracked the man down to Spanish Island and he planned to snatch him and recover the goods. But he needed help and he would to pay ten thousand dollars to get it.

Wellons' eyes widened and fixed on Marley's for a few seconds. "Who is this person that stole from you?"

"His name is Simon Albury. Like me, he is from the Bahamas."

"That's funny. A guy I know use to fish with him. He says Simon screwed him out of a big prize worth a lot of money. But I'm gonna talk to our friend before I give you an answer. I'll let you know what he says."

"Just remember this," Marley said. "We're talking about a lot of money and I don't deal in fun and games. Make sure he understands that."

"Meet us tomorrow at the Chart House. About eight o'clock." Wellons pointed, "It's right over there. If he's interested, he'll join us."

The meeting the next evening produced a large tab but the deputy didn't show up. Marley became impatient with his two guests and got up to leave when a waitress whispered something to Wellons. He relayed the information. "He's in the parking lot. He wants to see you now."

The three men walked outside to an unmarked, black Crown Victoria. The window opened on the driver's side and Wellons looked inside. "This is him, Sonny."

The door swung open, but the man remained seated behind the wheel. Marley's first impression of Sonny Fletcher was that of an unkempt adult who never grew out of his baby face. His gut fell over his belt and his chin drooped over a spotted shirt.

In contrast, and in spite of his beard and bald pate, Marley was well groomed. He wore khaki slacks that were sharply creased and a freshly laundered shirt. Topsider deck shoes rounded out the look of a casual yachtsman.

"What can I do for you, Mr. Marley?"

"Well, Sheriff, I'm from the Bahamas. I'm here because a man who stole some goods from me is hiding out in the area. His name is Simon Albury and I aim to get him and to reclaim my property."

"What kind of goods?"

"I deal in recreational products."

"Why are we having this conversation?"

"I thought perhaps you could deflect any unnecessary attention, for a price of course."

Marley looked deep into Fletcher's eyes. The man had no conscience. That was good. Men like that were predictable.

Fletcher extricated his bulk from the car, "Wellons, you and Sykes stay here. We're taking a walk."

"You can cut the bullshit right now, Marley. What do you take me for, an idiot? Recreational products, my red ass."

"Well, occasionally I deal in other commodities."

"Fuckin' A you do, and I bet it's all the time. You say you came from the Bahamas on a boat?"

"That's right."

"How long did it take you to get here?"

"We stopped at Walker's Cay to refuel. From there it took just under eleven hours."

"Who is we?"

"I've got a mate."

"Show me this boat."

"Follow me. I'm in a transient slip just past the ramp."

In the dark, the black-hulled craft was all but invisible, but lights burned in her salon behind drawn curtains. Marley rapped on a side window with his knuckles before stepping into the cockpit. "Come aboard, Sheriff."

"I ain't the sheriff, I'm his deputy."

"Sorry, my mistake."

Fletcher managed to step over the gunwale and had both feet on the deck when Owen Marshall opened the salon door and stepped out. His bulging eyes seemed to jump from their sockets as they took in every detail about him, particularly the uniform and gun belt.

Marley handed him some bills. "Go and have yourself a couple of beers. Be back in an hour. Come in, Deputy, and have a seat."

Fletcher sidled through the door and plopped down on a couch in the spacious salon.

"What's wrong with his eyes?"

"He's got a condition known as Graves' disease. It runs in his family."

"Well shit, he's one ugly son of a bitch."

Marley switched off the TV. "Can I offer you a drink?"

"Bourbon on the rocks, Maker's Mark if you got it."

"I've got it right here." Marley fixed the drink and handed it to Fletcher. He opened a Kalik for himself.

"Nice boat, Marley. What's a rig like this cost?"

"Equipped as she is, about four hundred thousand."

Fletcher whistled. "That's a lot of recreational products."

"Well Deputy, the numbers add up in a hurry. The goods Albury stole from me are worth six hundred thousand. I'm willing to pay five percent for someone to keep things under the radar until I get Albury and the goods out of here. That amounts to thirty thousand for doing nothing."

Fletcher extended his empty glass for a refill. "Yeah, well single digits don't float my boat. Ten percent or I'm walking out of here now, and I'll be watching you."

Marley had underestimated the man. He was more cunning than he looked. He handed him a fresh drink. "What sort of protection can I expect for ten percent?"

"I'm in charge of this part of the county. I say who gets assigned here and who don't. I say when we check into something and when we don't. The Sheriff looks to me to let him know what's going on. He don't have time to come runnin' every time some asshole steals a car."

"Does that mean that if someone reported suspicious activity it would be your call whether to follow up or to disregard the tip?"

"That's exactly what it means."

"Well Deputy, I think we can do business. The man I'm after stays over on Spanish Island? I'm told people over there mind their own business, but I need a place that's out of the way where I can persuade him to give up the goods. Any suggestions?"

"There's a place on the water over there with an old dock and a shed. It's called the Campbell property. It's right on a bend in the creek. As I recall, there's no close neighbors. No one will bother you there."

"Tell me Deputy, can Wellons and Sykes be trusted?"

"Yeah, but they're both dumber than shit. Don't tell 'em anything they don't need to know."

"Is there anything else I should know about doing business with you?"

"Just this Marley, if we got a deal, it's a deal. The first time you try to fuck me over will be your last. I'll nail your balls to a piling at low tide, you and that pop-eyed freak you call a mate. Do you get my drift?"

"You make yourself very clear, Deputy, but while we're on the subject, you should know that I have silent partners. They are powerful men with unlimited resources. They have long memories and no mercy. If I were the subject of their wrath, I would kill myself before they could find me. Do you grasp the meaning of what I just said?"

"Yeah, big deal. I know how to deal with assholes."

Marley despised the man. Fletcher was a pig. He would enjoy killing him, and he would do it slowly, but that pleasure would have to wait. He would deal with Simon Albury first.

The deputy finished his drink in two gulps. "Give me some time and I'll find out what I can about this Albury guy. Don't do anything until I get back to you.

Wellons arranged for Fletcher to meet with Tyler Merrill the next day, and the deputy learned all that he knew about Simon. A day later Fletcher returned to the marina. He banged on the side of the boat until Owen appeared at the salon door. "Where's Marley?"

"He went to the ship's store." The mate pointed to the marina building.

"Fletcher grunted, "I'll look for him up there." He stared at the man's eyes for a second before leaving. Marley had a dock cart full of supplies when Fletcher met him at the top of the ramp.

Fletcher eyed the contents that included duct tape and a coil of rope.

"I got some news for you. Your boy lives with a woman named Twilight Pinckney. She delivers the mail over there. He fishes a boat for Henry Parker and he's out three or four days a week. He don't spend much money, and he don't leave the island except to fish."

Fletcher did not mention that it was a stroke of luck that Simon and Twilight were lovers. It presented an unexpected but very welcome opportunity. If he played his cards right, he might get Marley to get rid of her for him. Then it would be just a matter of time before her property on the river became available. David Trask would owe him big time for that.

Marley was surprised but pleased to learn that Simon lived simply. The bulk of the drugs or the money must be intact. A plan began to form in his mind. Wellons and Sykes would snatch the man early one morning before he left to go fishing. They would take him from the boat and bring him to the Campbell place where Marley would have the privacy to work him over. After Marley recovered his property, Owen could have his fun. It would be the last and longest day of Simon's life. Marley thought he might even take photos to spread around back home. No one would double cross him again.

CHAPTER TWENTY-NINE

Four passenger utility carts had become the preferred mode of transportation on the island. Well-suited to dirt roads, they could also run on paths through the woods. Unlike motor vehicles they were exempt from registration and from the unpopular personal property tax. County or state taxes of any kind were anathema to Spanish Islanders who got little in return. There were no paved roads, no schools and no fire protection or police services, although most residents saw no need for the latter.

In observance of Ettie's birthday, Kathleen took her for a ride around the island. Ettie loved riding in the cart. She smiled and waved at birds and squirrels and seemed to delight in the bumpy sojourn. She had moved in with Cooper and Kathleen a few months after their marriage. Kathleen happily cared for her mother-in-law, and the older woman delighted in her attention.

They went first to the beach at the south end where the waves sparkled in the late fall afternoon. Gulls swooped low to catch the crackers they threw in the air and Ettie beamed and clapped her hands. Next they rode down Eagle Point Road— basically a wide dirt path bordered by maritime forest. Kathleen drove past Twilight's place on the way to the sparsely populated back side. They came out on the old logging road that ran the length of the island and ended at what remained of a pier where barges once loaded timber.

Kathleen noticed a pleasure boat tied up at the dock. No one had used the place in years. She steered closer to get a better look, stopping next to a rundown building that had served as an office for the timber operation. When she stepped out of the cart a voice startled her.

"This is private property, Missy. Get back in your cart and leave." The words came from a black man with a funny accent whose eyes seemed to pop from their sockets. Ettie was disturbed by the tone of the man's voice. She frowned and held Sunny close to her bosom.

Kathleen became incensed. "Who are you? This place belongs to the Campbell family."

"None of your business who I am. Get back in the cart and go."

Kathleen started back towards the cart when she noticed that Ettie's eyes were frozen on the door to the office. She turned in time to see a second man, a white, disappear inside. Kathleen saw only the back of his bald head, but Ettie had fixed his image in her mind.

As they drove home Kathleen could not stop thinking about the first man's rudeness. Who was he? What use would anyone have for that old place? Who was the second man, and why would he try to hide? With difficulty, she put it out of her mind. She would tell Cooper about it later. For now she intended to see that Ettie's birthday party would be a happy one. As her mother-in-law rocked in a chair on the deck, Kathleen busied herself with the preparations.

Everyone had their fill of deviled crabs and barbecued shrimp, hush puppies and home-made slaw. White corn on the cob and sliced tomatoes with basil and vinegar added to the feast.

Uncle Henry and Cooper were enjoying the last traces of sunlight on the deck when Henry extracted one of the Cohibas from his pocket. He ran the cigar back and forth under his nose savoring the richness of the aged leaves.

As she cleared the table Kathleen remembered the encounter earlier in the day. "By the way, when Ettie and I went riding today, we came back past the old Campbell place. A big boat was tied up at the dock. We stopped for a closer look but a man told us to leave. He was very rude. Another man ducked out of sight before I could see his face. What would anyone want with that old place?"

"Beat's me," said Henry. "The way that channel's silted in you can't get in or out with any kind of commercial boat except at high tide. You don't suppose they would try to develop it do you Cooper?"

"That wouldn't make sense, there's not enough acreage on that tract to make it worthwhile."

"Well, it seemed strange to me and I thought I'd mention it. Is everyone ready for the cake?"

"Kathleen, honey," said Melanie, "it's a good thing we don't eat here more often. We'd all belong in the circus."

"Well it's Ettie's birthday. We can diet tomorrow."

"I just thought of something," Cooper said. "Coming back from Savannah last week I passed a sheriff's skiff going south. When I looked back it turned into the Campbell place."

Henry said, "Well, it ain't our property and it ain't our business. We'd just as well forget about it."

"Henry," Melanie fixed him with a cold stare, "the Campbells were fine neighbors and good friends of your Daddy's. You can't just ignore something like that."

"Honey, the Campbells are long gone and their house burned down over ten years ago. Their kin own the property, I guess, but we ain't seen them in a coon's age. Besides what harm can anyone do to a run-down old dock house and some rotten pilings in the mud? It just ain't our concern."

Kathleen came back with the cake. "You know, Regina Driessen told me she heard a boat speeding through the inlet one night last week. She said it reminded her of the old days when the rum-runners used to sneak in, but I thought most islanders were teetotalers back then"

"Most were, but they didn't have no moral hang-ups about it neither." Henry shifted the unlit cigar in his teeth. "The smugglers had big fast boats that would run offshore to meet a coastal freighter. Then they'd bring the booze in here and dole it out to smaller boats. A lot of the locals made extra money helping to transfer the loads."

"You don't suppose someone's trying to smuggle whiskey to the island?"

"Naw, repeal took all the profit out of that and put most of the moonshiners out of business too. But I still say what goes on at the Campbell place is none of our business."

CHAPTER THIRTY

Wellons and Sykes arrived at the Landing just after five a.m. They secured their skiff to the outboard side of *Blind Pig* and crept over the side. They were careful not to make a sound until they knew they were alone. A dim light in the deck house provided all the illumination they needed to reconnoiter. They would ambush Simon as he came aboard. Now they just had to wait.

Sykes broke the silence. "I don't like this Craig. This is kidnapping. It's federal. I don't need the FBI on my ass."

"Relax. All we're gonna do is deliver the guy to Marley. He don't know we're here and we'll jump him. Nothin' to it."

"Yeah? Well he's a big son of a bitch. What if something goes wrong?"

"Ain't nothin' gonna go wrong. One tap with this billy and he'll go down like a bag of cement."

Sykes shook his head. "I don't know, I don't need no FBI . . ."

"What about that woman on Dolphin Island? That was murder. It don't get no worse than that. They didn't come after us for that did they?"

"No, but they thought she died natural."

"That's because we planned it that way. Sonny told us how to do it. Remember, he told you to hold her arms and legs so she didn't bang them up? Then I just had to hold the pillow over her face. Easy. Nothin' to it. Plannin', that's the key to everything."

Sykes sat quietly for a moment. "Well, I'll just be glad when it's over."

Simon arrived at five. He and his mate, Duane Driessen, had readied *Blind Pig* the previous afternoon. They topped off the fuel and fresh water tanks and made sure that the freezer contained plenty of bait. They stocked the refrigerator with enough food for a week in case they stayed out longer than expected.

Simon walked through the door into the deck house and plugged in the coffee maker. He started forward to start the engine when something crashed into the back of his head. Simon dropped to his knees, momentarily stunned. In an instant the men pounced on him. A strip of duct tape covered his mouth, another went over his eyes, and they taped his hands behind him. Someone splashed water in his face and forced him to his feet. They pushed him towards the stern where his legs were bound together.

The two men manhandled him up and over the gunwale and then half lowered and half dropped him into a smaller boat. When the outboard cranked his captors angled away from *Blind Pig* and reversed direction back into Spanish Creek.

He tried to ask "who are you, where are you taking me," but only a series of grunts escaped the tape. The man closest to him gave him a sharp backhand and told him to shut up.

In less than ten minutes he heard the engine throttle back and he sensed they were turning to port. A minute later he felt a jolt as the skiff bumped against a dock.

Then he heard a voice. "Well, well, Mr. Albury. What a pleasure it is to see you again. Take off the blindfold," the voice commanded.

One of the men ripped the tape from his eyes and unbound his legs. Simon looked up. In the early light he could just make out the face of Lucas Marley peering down at him.

"Stand up," ordered one of his captors. Simon rose unsteadily. Hands gripped his arms and pushed him forward. "Get up on the dock. Hurry up."

"Let's go inside shall we," Marley gestured with his hand.

Simon could make out a dark one-story structure at the end of the dock as they pushed him towards it. The windows had been covered with cardboard, but lanterns illuminated the space inside.

"Have a seat won't you Simon?' Marley indicated a single wooden chair at the side of the room. One of the men ushered him towards it but Simon jerked free from his grasp and butted into him. As the man sprawled to the floor, someone felled Simon with a chop to his neck. He collapsed on the floor. Several pairs of rough hands manhandled him into the chair, splashed water in his face, and tore the tape from his mouth. Marley dismissed the two men who had abducted him. "Go on back to the marina. I'll talk to you later."

They were glad to leave and hurried out of the building.

Marley slapped Simon's face. "Look at me. You stole my boat and my goods. I want my property back and I intend to get it, whatever it takes. You're intelligent, so you must understand that you're not going to leave here alive. Don't make it hard on yourself? Just tell me what I want to know and that will be the end of it."

Dazed, Simon looked up into a pair of bulging eyes.

Marley continued. "This man is Owen Marshall. He is an expert in the art of persuasion, and he's passionate about his work. Now, tell me, what did you do with the boat and the drugs?"

"I was high-jacked. They took the duffels and blew up the boat."

Marley looked at Owen and nodded. In an instant Simon felt more pain than he had ever experienced. Owen's fingers were clamped on a nerve at the base of his neck. He gasped.

"That was just a little sample, Simon. Owen is a true sadist. The more he can make you suffer, the more excited he gets. It's a sexual thing with him. He'll get the truth out of you sooner or later. Why do you want to go through this?"

"I'm telling you the truth. Some Latinos sneaked up without lights and boarded me. They took the drugs and blew up the boat."

After another glance from Marley, Owen delivered a vicious kick to Simons left knee. The pain flashed through his nervous system and as he bellowed, Owen's fingers dug into his shoulder again. Simon blacked out.

The torment continued but Simon could not tell Marley what he wanted to hear. As the day wore on Marley became exasperated. He had Owen bind Simon's hands more securely and tie a length of rope around his ankles. Together, they dragged him to an opening in the floor. The rope ran through a block and tackle fastened to an overhead beam. They lowered him into the water below so that his head and shoulders were submerged. He hung suspended for a full minute, thrashing like a hog-tied bull before they pulled him from the water.

Marley slapped his face, "now do you have something to tell me?"

Simon gagged and spit up some water but said nothing.

Marley slapped him again harder, "answer me."

"I told you, someone high-jacked the boat. I didn't steal your drugs."

"Put him back in the water, Owen. He's not paying attention."

This time, Simon didn't thrash. He didn't move at all, and now it was dark under the dock. His tormentors could not see below Simon's bound feet. The tide had ebbed and his mouth and nose were barely six inches below the surface. No sound came from below. Simon held his breath for as long as possible before doubling up to gulp air. Marley watched nervously. The last thing he needed was to drown the man before finding the drugs or the money.

"Now, pull him up now," he ordered.

Owen wrestled with the rope until Simon's legs and torso appeared above the opening. Just then the door swung open from the dock, and Fletcher came in.

"Well, well, havin' a little party, are we?"

"He's being stubborn," replied Marley.

The three men watched in surprise as Simon's head cleared the opening. He settled quietly on the plywood that had been pushed over the hole again. A fiddler crab left its hiding place in his ear and scurried away.

Fletcher watched him intently. "He's a mess ain't he? His old fishing buddy said he's real tight with that Pinckney woman. I wonder if he gave the stuff to her for safe keeping. Could be he don't have it after all."

Fletcher had already planned how to spend his sixty thousand. He didn't want it to slip through his fingers because Marley screwed it up.

"You need to go snatch the woman."

"How do you propose that we do that?"

"Get that watch off his wrist and take it to her. Tell her he's hurt and needs help. She lives on Eagle Point Road. There's a Post Office jeep parked out front. The house is white with blue doors and windows."

"Alright, Owen will go. How does he get there from here?" Marley asked.

Fletcher drew a crude map in the dust on the floor and gestured with a finger, "Go over here to the fish company office. It's almost dark and there won't be no one around. There's usually two or three carts in the storage room. Take one and go get her."

"How long will it take him?" Marley asked.

"Fifteen or twenty minutes if he don't get lost."

Marley looked at Owen, "Get his watch."

Simon tried to twist away but the man was too fast and too strong. He pulled the watch off, snapping the band, and backhanded Simon for resisting.

In the gathering gloom, lightening danced in clouds to the west as muted thunder punctured the stillness. Twilight paced. Concern consumed her. Simon had simply vanished. No one had seen him since he left her that morning, and *Blind Pig* still lay in her slip. When Duane arrived at five-thirty Simon was not aboard. Duane waited fifteen or twenty minutes before leaving to look for him. He went first to the storeroom and the office, and then to the deck at Wanda's, but he found no trace of the man.

Twilight knew something had to be very wrong. He must be somewhere on the island. But where would he go? Could he have wandered into the woods? Could he be sick? He would never do something like this as a joke. The questions tormented her.

Cooper had gone to Savannah. She had nowhere else to turn. On impulse she decided to visit Kathleen and Ettie. Kathleen greeted her at the door, "Hi Twi, come on in. Cooper's not home yet and we get lonely."

"Thanks. I'm worried sick about Simon. It's like he disappeared into thin air." She told Kathleen what she knew and crossed the room to give Ettie a hug.

"What do you mean disappeared? When did you see him last?"

"This morning, when he left to go fishing. When Duane got to the boat he found the coffee plugged in, but no trace of Simon. He hasn't come home and no one has seen him. He's got to be on the island somewhere. But what if he's sick or hurt?"

"Twi, it has to be a misunderstanding. Are you sure he didn't go to the mainland for some reason?"

"Where would he go? And for what?"

Kathleen reached for the phone. "I'll call Henry. Maybe he knows something."

Twilight said, "I saw him an hour ago. He hasn't seen Simon all day."

She sank into the couch and brushed a tear from her eye. Ettie approached her and reached for her hand. She pulled gently.

"She wants to show you her room," said Kathleen. "We painted it last week. It's much cheerier. Come on, let's go look."

The three climbed the stairs to the second floor bedroom. It looked warm and inviting. Bright yellow paint made the space seem larger. The windows were treated with checked yellow, blue and white chintz curtains that Kathleen had crafted on her sewing machine. A huge canopied bed with a quilted spread and fluffy pillows occupied one side of the room. On the other Cooper had built shelves to accommodate knick knacks—sea shells, small framed photographs, and the doll collection.

The little figures were perched like a gallery of spectators. On the top row were likenesses of Twilight, Cooper, Kathleen, Melanie and Uncle Henry, and a host of other locals. The ones on the second shelf were mostly celebrities and sports figures, but one in particular caught Twilight's eye. It was the image of a bald man with a bushy brown beard. She shivered involuntarily. Simon had told her about Lucas Marley, the man who hired him to deliver *Abaco Belle*. The doll matched his description exactly.

Twilight picked it off the shelf. "Kathleen, who is this?"

"I don't know, but she made that one the day after her birthday. It might be the man she saw at the Campbell place."

Kathleen told her of the outing on the cart. "I never saw the second man, but she did."

"Oh, my God, what if they have come after Simon? Can I borrow this?"

"Sure, but what good will that do?"

"I might need it to help Simon. I've got to go. I'll call you later."

"Where are you going? It's dark and it's going to rain. Don't you hear the thunder?"

"I'll be all right. Thanks."

Cooper arrived home just after dark. He bolted up the stairs as the first drops of rain dimpled the sand in the driveway.

"Hi, I'm home."

Kathleen sat on the deck with his mother. "Oh, Honey, I'm so glad you're here."

She explained about Simon and told him Twilight had gone to find him.

"Where did she go?"

"One of the dolls upstairs fit the description of the man who hired Simon to deliver the boat to Florida. He could be the one your mother saw at the Campbell place."

"But where did she go?"

"I don't know. She's pretty upset."

Cooper dialed Twilight's number but the phone rang unanswered. He donned a rain jacket. "I've got to find her. I'll try the Landing. Maybe she's there."

"Let me come with you."

"Honey it's raining, and we shouldn't leave my mother alone. This is just some crazy mix up. I'll be home shortly."

Cooper went straight to Wanda's but found it locked and dark. She must have closed early, but he found the door to the storeroom open. He stepped out of his cart and walked towards the entrance.

"Uncle Henry, you in there?" he called. No response.

"Uncle Henry," he tried again.

He was right in front of the door when Owen lunged at him with an old swordfish harpoon. Cooper side-stepped, but stumbled and fell backwards in the wet dirt. The man recovered and came at him again, aiming the pike at his throat.

The point stuck in the mud as Cooper rolled out of the way and grabbed the shaft, wrestling with the other man for control. He was back on his feet when Owen kicked wildly at his groin, but the length of the weapon kept him out of range. Owen dropped his end and reached into his pocket. His hand came out with a knife that flicked open at the touch of a button. Cooper quickly turned the shaft so that it pointed at his attacker. He backed into the glow of an outside corner light but tripped on a root and sprawled on the ground.

Owen seized the opportunity. His eyes puffed out as he flew at Cooper with his knife in front of him. Cooper shuffled backwards with his arms and legs. With one hand he raised the harpoon. As a flash of lightening blinded him, Owen fell on the point. His eyes opened even wider as a grunt exploded from his lips, followed by rasping gasps as he tumbled sideways. His breathing became weaker and then stopped altogether. Cooper's mind raced. Where had the man come from?

He grabbed a flashlight from his cart and shined it at the form on the ground. The half-closed eyes still bulged from their sockets. It was one of the men he had seen at the fuel dock a few days earlier. Could he be linked to Simon's disappearance? He thought suddenly of the larger man. Could he be on the island, too?

He searched the body for some clue. There was no wallet, just a few folded bills and a handkerchief. But when he reached into the left front pocket he discovered Simon's watch. Now he knew his friend was in trouble. Cooper ran to his cart and steered down the road to the Campbell place.

Twilight rushed home with the doll. The lights of her cart probed the darkness at the sides of the road. She could hear and feel the thunder as the storm marched eastward from the mainland across vast stretches of marsh. She collected several items from the table in the front room and tossed them in a pillow case. Then she hurried back outside and headed straight for the woods and the sanctum.

Shrubbery snatched at her as she bounced over the rough path. A fox, fixed by the headlights, stood frozen in her path. Slowing momentarily, she spoke softly.

"Get yo se'f home critter. Go on, git."

The animal did as she bid and disappeared into the brush.

Except for the rumble of thunder all was still. Not a peep from a tree frog, nor a whisper of breeze could be heard, and the forest canopy looked as still as a painting. The clouds of the coming storm filtered the moonlight, yet an eerie luminescence penetrated the circle protected by the great oaks.

She went straight to the shell altar and spread the lace cloth on the rough surface. After smoothing it with her hands she placed silver candlesticks with black tapers at either side. As the wicks flickered to life, a flash of lightening lit up the forest. She counted the seconds until she heard the boom. The storm was getting closer. She would have to hurry. She placed the likeness of Marley on the altar and arranged the other items in front of her.

She sprinkled goofer dust in a circle around the doll and tied a hat pin and a piece of blue root together with a black ribbon. She reached for a vial of red fluid but hesitated. A sudden chill breeze gave her goose bumps as thunder rumbled from across the river. She was terrified about calling up the Spirits, but she had no choice. She dipped the pin into the thick red substance and held it near the flame until the coating congealed.

With the ends of the ribbon, she tied the blood-tipped pin and the blue root to the torso of the doll. She blew out the candles and swept the other items back into the sack. The smell of ozone filled the air as she hurried back to her cart and drove straight to the dock house.

Twilight parked well away from the old pier and continued on foot. Rain pelted her face as she neared the structure. It appeared empty and dark, but as she watched, the door opened. In the light from inside she could see two men coming out. One wore a uniform and gun belt. She recognized him as Deputy Fletcher. The second man relieved himself on a bush. He wore a beard, and she knew it had to be Marley.

Her mind raced. What was Fletcher doing here? What could he have to do with Simon's disappearance? What could he be doing with Marley?

CHAPTER THIRTY-ONE

When Owen did not return after half an hour, Fletcher became impatient. "He's just a damn nigger. Why the hell did you send him? You shoulda gone yourself."

"Owen is perfectly capable of borrowing a cart and dealing with a woman. He'll be here any minute."

"Yeah, well I ain't got all night. This business should'a been done by now."

A flash of lightening and an almost simultaneous crack of thunder rattled the rickety building.

Fletcher's eyes darted to the roof. "Shit, that was close."

Twilight crouched under a tree and waited, unsure of what to do next. She had crept to within a few yards of the dock house when the door flew open again. This time, she could see Simon lying bound on the floor inside. Marley and Fletcher walked towards the front of the building, looking for any sign of Owen.

She pulled the doll from the pocket of her jacket but hesitated momentarily. She thought of the warnings of the Spirits in her dreams so long ago. Her hands shook as she punctured Marley's likeness with the blood-tipped pin.

She watched as a look of surprise crossed Marley's face. He reached behind him as if to pluck something from his back. His eyes opened wide as he leaned against the wall of the building.

Then she heard the sound of feet running through the wet underbrush. Three dark forms rushed past her towards the building. Fletcher saw them coming and made for the woods, but Marley turned and stumbled back through the door. They caught him just inside. He fell to the floor and scurried frantically on hands and knees to escape them. Now the intruders were on top of him, snapping and snarling. He held his arms in front of his face as he bumped into Simon's prone figure. Simon rolled on his side and managed to get Marley in a headlock with legs that were still bound at the ankles. He twisted sharply and snapped the man's neck.

Twilight ran through the door. At her command the dogs backed away. She pulled Simon away from Marley's body and cut the tape that bound him. She wiped the blood from his face with the bottom of her blouse and held his head to her bosom as she rocked back and forth on her knees. Then Cooper arrived. He jumped from his cart and rushed through the door. He struggled to understand the scene in front of him.

"What the hell happened here?" he asked.

"Dat man, he daid, an' Simon, he hurt real bad and Cooper, Depity Fletcher, he out dere."

"Fletcher, here? Where is he?"

She began to calm down. Her speech slowed and the dialect began to disappear.

"He run in de woods when de dogs come. He hidin' from the dogs."

Cooper looked at Twilight, "Where did the dogs come from?"

"I needed help. I called for help."

He noticed the little figure on the floor next to her but said nothing.

Cooper said, "I'll pull the cart up to the door. It will be easier for him."

Fletcher perched in a tree eight feet off the ground. He would have had no chance against three dogs. He decided to stay put for the moment. Twilight had gone inside, and now Hamilton was here. He'd have to get rid of him, too, if there was still a chance of turning up the money. With Cooper out of the way they could work on the woman until Simon gave it up.

But where was Owen? And what happened to Marley? He watched as Twilight appeared at the door with the dogs. It looked as if she talked to them before they loped off towards the Landing. This was his chance. He'd have to get close enough to get a clean shot at Hamilton. He climbed out of the tree.

Cooper emerged from the dock house and started towards his cart when Fletcher drew his gun and aimed with both hands.

A hoarse voice shattered the stillness. "Look out, he's got a gun."

Cooper dropped instinctively as Fletcher fired three times. Two bullets smacked into a tree just inches from his head. Then a rifle cracked from the opposite direction. Fletcher's gun flew out of his hand. He grabbed at his left his shoulder where he had been hit and lurched towards the door. When he saw

Marley's still form lying on the floor inside he bolted. He turned and ran towards his launch at the end of the dock.

Cooper saw him stumbling towards his launch. Years of hatred for the man welled up in him. Images of Kathleen's rape and of Jeannie's battered face flashed through his mind. He sprang to his feet and went after him.

Fletcher untied the lines and tumbled into the launch. He had just pulled away from the dock when Cooper leapt into the cockpit. Fletcher reached into his boot for a backup pistol but Cooper managed to grab his arm before he could take aim. As they struggled, Fletcher fell against the throttle. The launch surged ahead at top speed.

The man was incredibly strong. With just one good arm he gradually twisted the muzzle towards Cooper's midsection. Cooper punched Fletcher with his free hand, and he seemed to weaken, but he still had a firm grip on the gun. Cooper still could not wrest the pistol from his hand, but now he managed to twist it towards him. He heard a loud pop, and Fletcher slumped to the deck. Blood seeped from a hole in the bottom of his chin.

Cooper stopped the boat before it ran aground on the opposite bank. He dragged Fletcher's body away from the console before turning and steering back to the old dock. After tying up he took a last look at his nemesis. On impulse he stepped back into the launch and snatched Fletcher's badge from his shirt before jamming it between the man's jaws.

"That's for Pooch," he said.

His mind raced. Who had shot Fletcher? Who had shouted the warning? The words played over and over in his mind. "Look out, he's got a gun." It was the voice of a woman and vaguely familiar.

Suddenly, he knew whose it was.

Cooper jumped from the launch and ran to the edge of the woods, "Mom, where are you? Mother?"

"I'm here," a weak voice responded. Cooper followed the sound through the darkness to Kathleen's cart. Ettie sat in the passenger seat. He put his arms around her.

"Mom, you spoke. I heard your voice."

"I had to warn you. I just had to. I couldn't kill you too."

Large tears formed and streamed down her cheeks. She sobbed as Cooper struggled with what she had said.

"What do you mean? You didn't kill anyone."

She wiped her eyes and looked at him in desperation.

"I killed your father. I asked him to teach me to drive the tractor. We were laughing and I wasn't paying attention. When I hit a stump the tractor rolled over. I did it. I killed him."

"Mom," Cooper held her head against his chest, "it was an accident. Don't you understand? I can't believe you blamed yourself for that."

She sobbed, "You have his mouth and you have his eyes. I love you. I couldn't bear to lose you, too."

He held her tightly as Kathleen appeared at his side. She had a lantern in one hand and a rifle in the other. She had heard Ettie's words. Her eyes showed surprise and something else—the same expression that was on her face the night that Fletcher raped her.

"He tried to kill you" she said. Tears ran down her face as he pulled her close. "What happened to him?" she asked.

"He had another gun. We were struggling when it went off. He's dead."

The three were locked in an embrace when Ettie's head suddenly dropped. Cooper lifted her chin and looked into her half-closed eyes. Only then did they noticed the small hole on the front of her yellow rain jacket.

"Oh, my God," Kathleen screamed. Her fingers struggled to undo the zipper. A dark, wet spot covered the front of Ettie's blouse.

"She's been shot. Oh, dear God."

Cooper remembered that Fletcher had fired three shots, but only two bullets hit the tree.

Kathleen reached for Ettie's wrist and felt for a pulse. She could find none. She put her ear to the woman's breast but could not detect a heartbeat. Tears ran down her face as she looked at Cooper. He picked up his mother's small form and rocked it as he would a child. He held his face against the top of her head and whispered, "Oh Mom, Mom, please don't leave us now. When he looked into Kathleen's eyes she shook her head.

"She's gone."

Twilight appeared in the dim circle of light.

"Simon will be alright in time, maybe a couple of weeks," she said.

She looked at them, searching their faces. "What's wrong with your mother?"

They did not have to tell her. She saw the blood on Ettie's dress and she understood.

She went to Cooper and stroked his mother's hair. "Oh my po' baby. My po' lil' baby. God fo'give me."

"She talked to me, Twi. She said she loved me." Cooper all but choked on the words. He fell to his knees, and the next sound that left his lips was a pitiful howl that filled the dark void around them. "Why? Why? Oh God, why now?"

A powerful lantern switched on and fixed them in a pool of light. Ben Washington stepped out of the trees. He cradled a shotgun in his arms.

"I hear shots. Wha's goin' on here?"

Ben shined his light on the cart and Ettie's still form. The blood on her blouse was apparent.

"Oh Lawd, tell me she ain't dead."

Through her tears Kathleen nodded, "We've lost her."

Ben was dumbfounded. "Wha' happen?"

Cooper stammered, relating everything about the series of events. Ben listened intently, shaking his head and muttering, "Lawd, Lawd". When Cooper finished he looked at his old friend.

"Ben, will you help me?

"You know I will. What we got to do?"

Cooper took a deep breath. "We've got to get rid of the bodies."

"Well, how we do dat?"

"The sheriff's launch is tied up at the dock. We can put them in the cuddy cabin and sink the thing offshore."

"Oh, Lawd."

"We'll have to work fast. We have to get it done by daybreak."

Through her tears Twilight said, "I'll help Kathleen. We will take your Momma home."

"Twilight," Ben said, "tell Charisse I ain't be home directly."

She nodded her assent. Twilight drove, and Kathleen steadied Ettie's form as they started off towards Ben's place. They stopped first at The Landing where Twilight walked to the deck. Lamps from the dock illuminated the water below.

"I ain't had no choice, I ain't know what else to do," she said to no one.

She pulled Marley's likeness from a pocket and tossed it into the water. For several seconds it swirled in an eddy before slipping into the tide. She watched until it disappeared.

The night was pregnant with humidity. Insects of every description sang, chirped, and flitted in the soft light as muted rumbles of thunder followed the flickering of lightening far to the east. Tiny splashes of shrimp and the call of an owl were the only other sounds. Legions of fiddler crabs and snails burrowed into the exposed pluff mud, and the air filled up with its redolence.

Twilight turned away as the little effigy twisted in the current and disappeared from sight.

"I had no choice," she said again.

CHAPTER THIRTY-TWO

Ben and Cooper dragged Fletcher's body forward into the cuddy cabin. Next they went back to the dock house for Marley. He was a big man but not as heavy as Fletcher. They removed the cardboard from the windows and the rope and duct tape. After a final look around with Ben's light they were satisfied they had left no evidence. They returned to the launch and eased away from the dock.

"What about runnin' lights?" Ben asked.

"Too risky," Cooper replied. They made the ten minute run in darkness and tied up behind *Different Drummer*. Cooper climbed aboard to find an insulated fish bag.

They walked up the ramp to the storeroom and found Owen where he had fallen. His body fit into the bag with room to spare. They would leave no traces of blood on the dock. Cooper retrieved an axe from the storeroom as Ben hefted the fish bag over his shoulder. Owen's body joined the others in the launch.

Ben would pilot *Different Drummer* and Cooper would follow in the launch twenty-eight nautical miles offshore to a spot they knew as a dead zone. Anglers and divers would fish the area only out of ignorance or by mistake.

They would sink the launch and that would be the end of it. It was unlikely that anyone would ever discover the sunken boat or its gruesome cargo.

"Okay," Cooper said. "We're ready."

Ben turned to board *Different Drummer* when Cooper stopped him. "Ben, I don't know how I can ever thank you."

The big man smiled at him. "It ain't nuttin', man. Let's go."

Cooper watched his boat ease into the channel. The dock lights reflected off the ripples in the wake and appeared as columns of torches marching in opposite directions. A chuck-will's-widow squawked from somewhere nearby

In ten minutes the boats were clear of the inlet, and he closed the distance between them. Cooper checked his watch—12:15. It would take a little over an hour to reach their destination. His mind drifted back over the events of the last few hours. Tears welled in his eyes as he thought about his mother. He shook his head, uttered a long groan and steeled himself for the task at hand.

His thoughts turned to Simon. He hadn't even had time to speak with him. Cooper shook his head as he forced himself not to think about the man's ordeal. Suddenly he felt exhausted. He fought to keep his eyes open and focused on *Different Drummer*.

When it slowed and stopped, Cooper pulled alongside and threw a bow line that Ben secured to an aft cleat.

"Okay. Here we go."

With the light in one hand and the axe in the other Cooper swung at two thru-hull fittings until they broke off. Seawater gushed through, but it would take a while for the boat to sink. He turned and chopped at the hull until he had opened a hole roughly six inches square. The boat now filled rapidly. It began to roll side to side and the stern rode noticeably lower in the water.

Ben called, "C'mon Coop, climb up heah. Dat ting goin' down."

He scrambled off the sinking vessel and freed the bow line. Ben switched on the spreader lights, and both men watched as the launch spiraled into the depths. It disappeared from sight as Cooper dropped into his seat at the helm and reached for the controls.

"Let's go home," he said.

He shifted into gear, turned to the west and sat without a sound for several minutes before he inhaled a great quantity of air and sobbed. His frame shook with spasms as his grief escaped his lungs. Ben's big arm went around his shoulders.

"Dat's right, Cooper. Let it out. Let it all right out."

THE END

About the Author

Charles Thorn grew up in rural New York and served with the U.S. Army in Germany before enrolling at New York University. He later transferred to Northwestern's Medill School of Journalism and subsequently spent many years with Newsweek and Forbes magazines in New York and Atlanta before relocating to the Lowcountry of South Carolina.

Semi-retired, he now divides his time between writing and tourism. As a U.S. Coast Guard licensed captain, he ferries visitors across Calibogue Sound to conduct historical tours of remote Daufuskie Island, a Loyalist haven prior to the American Revolution. The island is rich in history and inspired the setting for much of his novel. It was there that he stumbled upon the complex issue of "heirs' property". Abuses are rampant, and unscrupulous lawyers and realtors make the situation worse. Because the predicament persists to this day, Thorn decided to bring it to light as the plot of his novel.

His second novel is in the works, and because of many readers' enthusiastic response to the main characters it will be a sequel.

He and his wife live on Hilton Head Island, S.C.